A Country Named Desire

Sabine J Saadeh

Published by SJ Saadeh, 2024.

A COUNTRY NAMED DESIRE

First edition. February 29, 2024.

Copyright © 2024 Sabine J Saadeh.

ISBN: 979-8224083800

Written by Sabine J Saadeh.

A Country Named Desire

Prologue

If the title of this novel is echoing a certain familiarity, you are not wrong. My inspiration for this story stems from the play "A Streetcar Named Desire" by Tennessee Williams.

For those who like me have wished to remain in Lebanon, the landscape of my country has become a sort of index of how to ride out catastrophes. You see, as a Lebanese that has lived through; a revolution, a financial downturn, the Covid-19 pandemic, the sixth largest accidental non-nuclear explosion by magnitude in history, a deliberate economic crisis that hasn't been experienced globally since the last one hundred and fifty years, a social isolation for a whole nation that is dwindling the civilized culture of the country and finally the Turkish-Syrian earthquake and its aftershocks that are a constant reminder of the larger mainshock on the fault and the sensitivity of human life, (take a deep breath) I couldn't help but feel the need to write down my thoughts about the whole experience.

Not to forget that all this happened in a mere three years.

Lebanon is a country that is ought to be called "Desire," it is a land of ancient and overlapping civilizations and a cradle of eighteen different religions. It is the nexus of historic trading routes and is situated at the crossroads of Asia, Africa and Europe. A conquest of intermarriages and displacements throughout history, and yet, it cannot help itself but attract the world even in misery.

The Lebanese have forgotten the notion of a street that might remind them of the loneliness of youth, the sight of a particular monument that might bring back the sting of getting fired from a job, a city center square that might remind them of their political fears, a dark alleyway that might recall the bliss of a love affair, a bar that evokes the memory of the privilege of being thoughtless, or a tree that would shelter them from the summer heat.

All a Lebanese person can remember is the success of a brief period of around fifteen years where economic growth was built on borrowed money. The ultimate use of a credit line that was not used to broaden the reach of democracy, but to restrict the freedom of thought!

This is a story about a country that can best be described by Tennesse Williams' play's most infamous line, the line that is uttered by one of his main characters at the very end of his theatrical masterpiece; "Whoever you are, I have always depended on the kindness of strangers."

Chapter 1: Blanche Dubois

January this year brought unexpected warmth that pervaded the air, reminiscent of the gentle embrace of spring. The need for heavy layers vanished, and was replaced by the mere necessity of a light jacket for an evening excursion. Amidst the urban landscape, the streets were adorned with bars aglow with dimmed lights, each emitting its own unique blend of music, creating a symphony of sound that intertwined with the murmur of people's voices. Amidst this vibrant scene, a perplexing question arises in the minds of passersby: How is it that these establishments are bustling with activity? Hasn't the country been labeled a failed state? Did not the recent report from the World Bank highlight that a staggering eighty percent of the population is languishing below the poverty line? Who are all these people?

But once settled in a bar and after a couple of drinks, one forgets all that and Beirut is back to being the cosmopolitan city of warm and easy intermingling. The casual acceptance of diversity and the open-minded sense of community is what has always been so attractive about it.

A strikingly handsome group of thirty and forty year olds are sitting haphazardly around a small orange resin table awkwardly placed on the sidewalk, brazenly watching the people make an effort not to bump into them as they walk up and down the street. More than half of the people in the place were looking at their phones while a few others were actually intermingling normally as humans ought to naturally do while laughing and teasing each other. It was not an expensive spot, but one of the few places with a radiator reliable enough to keep warm in winter, in case it actually gets very cold.

"Did you see the new meme about the new MPs?" a dark haired guy asks one of the women sitting beside him.

"No... I'm not really following the situation anymore!" she replies casually.

"Yes me too" a grayish haired man joins in.

The dark haired guy continues "Well it is about how one of the new MPs is against giving back people's money."

"Goodness, this nightmare is never going to end." The woman sitting on his other side says without removing her eyes from her phone.

Rolling to a stop on an over laden scooter a young thin teenager uneasily balances bags and a carton full of cans, plastic bottles and other recyclables mined from the trash, he then squats and lights a cigarette as he smiles at the group from the other side of the street. The entire bar was looking at him as he seemed to be waiting for someone else apparently, his eyes were a bit red and his clothes disheveled and dirty from a long day of dumpster diving, but he seemed content, more content than most of the people that were staring at him from across the street.

"So what are we going to do now?" the dark haired guy asks as he looked back at his friends,

"I have no idea, I guess forget about that money!" the gray haired man answers while sipping his beer and still looking at the young boy,

"I meant now, what are we going to do now after this place?" the dark haired guy chuckles.

The nonchalant woman says "I'm going home I'm very tired!"

While the woman that has an intimate relationship with her phone says "I'm in for whatever you feel like doing." She beams at the dark haired guy, and continues "also my cousin is here from the UK and she wants to experience Beirut after dark." She laughs flirtatiously.

"Beirut after dark? What does that even mean?" the gray haired man asks,

"Clubbing!" the woman answers curtly, "Isn't that what they used to call it in your days?"

"I'm not that older than you darling! So where are you planning on taking her?" he asks curiously,

"Mmmm...I guess The Warehouse!" she answers as she searches her phone even more enthusiastically.

"How old do you think?" the gray haired man asks,

"She's twenty-nine" the woman looks up from her phone

"I'm talking about the boy!" the gray haired man exclaims,

"Around thirteen," the dark haired guy answers and smiles at the boy,

"What boy?" the woman of the phone looks around curiously,

"This is how you are going to The Warehouse Haya?" the retiring woman asks.

Haya looks at her phone again, she had Instagram open on her phone, she looks at the photos of the place and then at her own clothes, her expression isn't as confident as her attitude.

"I thought it was casual!" She exclaims in disbelief.

"Well not tonight!" says the gray haired man

"It's Desire Night!" the dark haired guy strokes her free hand.

Haya giggles and finally looks up from her phone "it's a shame you are not joining Laura, if I didn't have my cousin here I would be going home too though."

"Laura always leaves at 11!" The dark haired guy exclaimed frustratingly.

"So where are we meeting your cousin?" the gray haired man asked.

"Here!" Haya replied as she glued her eyes again to her phone.

"How long does she need?" the dark haired guy asked.

"Ten minutes, she's just right here around the corner." Haya answered looking up at him warmly.

"Stay with us Laura until she comes." The gray haired man said graciously.

"Sure! And that will be 11:05, Sir Kamal." Laura laughed at the dark haired guy.

Kamal's social pedigree was not the kind that can be easily laughed at, but to Laura that never amounted to anything for her neither before the crisis and most certainly not now, and finally in 2023, some people were beginning to understand what that means or so she told herself.

Haya's cousin arrived, her appearance was completely incompatible with the place that her cousin and her friends were hanging out at. She was tall, slim and with a delicate beauty that made Kamal's eyes quiver with delight. Her outfit was glistening with black and gold material that made her look like she just jumped out of a magazine cover. Laura looked at her and couldn't help but feel a sting of jealousy, she didn't even stand up with the rest when the woman arrived at the table, but just smiled and nodded.

For many Lebanese adult women, the concept of heels, jewelry, and makeup has become a distant memory, let alone the idea of wearing shiny clothes. Ever since they began participating in demonstrations near Martyr's Square, their attire has transitioned to a sporty chic style. However, in light of the country's financial collapse, their clothing has become even more threadbare. In such a grim environment, those fortunate enough to afford new clothes often refrained from wearing them, as it would be seen as tactless.

"Well hello," the gray haired man told Haya's cousin as he remained standing to shake her hand, "my name is Malek."

"Rena." She said waving at the rest of the people that were sitting around the table.

To place things into perspective, Lebanon had already become like a fallen woman in society's eyes; the family fortune and estates are gone, there is no partner to rely on, the country suffers from a bad drinking problem and sexual impropriety. Lebanese society tries to cover that up poorly with social snobbery that has become totally outdated and is completely out of place. So the insecurity is ever present when a foreigner is admitted to a social group, as their perpetual panic about their fading lifestyles is exerted in their showy but cheap mannerisms.

"Excuse me, but I have to leave," Laura announced to the group, gracefully rising from her seat.

"Are you sure you don't want to join?" Just for a bit?" Haya pleaded, casting a doubtful look at Rena, who had now become the center of attention in Kamal's eyes.

Laura smiled at Haya, whose eyes were promising future confidences. "You'll tell me everything tomorrow," said Laura reassuring her friend that she will be there to listen.

"Goodbye gorgeous," Malek bid farewell to Laura as she elegantly moved away from the table.

Kamal didn't say anything and didn't even notice his friend leaving, but was eyeing Rena up and down brutishly. "So who is ready for some love?" he asked the group while smiling mischievously at his new prey.

INSIDE THE WAREHOUSE, people were being knocked against each other to navigate successfully to certain places inside the nightclub. As the four newcomers steered each other through the tumultuous atmosphere, Haya seized the opportunity to claim a nearby vacant chair. With slightly hunched shoulders and tightly pressed legs, she sought a moment of respite in the midst of the chaos.

Malek looked at Haya concerned, "Do you need the bathroom?" he asked her sweetly.

Haya smiled faintly, her eyes scanning the surroundings until they landed on the distant bar. "Oh no," she replied, "Malek, darling can you please fetch me a drink?" she tugged his arm lightly as he stood next her, pondering about the whereabouts of Kamal and Rena.

"Sure, stay here, I'll be right back," Malek told her with a hint of eagerness in his tone. He welcomed the excuse to explore the scene at the bar; leaving Haya momentarily as he ventured into the bustling crowd, curious about what awaited him there.

In that moment Rena bursts out of a nearby corner with Kamal, laughing and hugging him tightly every now and then. Haya looked at her cousin and could not help but gaze at her and take in their radiating energy of possible happy endings. Rena catches Haya staring at her from the corner of her eye and playfully drags Kamal towards her, creating a lively trio, through locked arms and hugs.

"So what are we drinking?" Rena's voice cut through the rhythmic tunes.

"Malek is getting me a gin and tonic." Haya answers back with a feverish vivacity. She then stood up abruptly and hurried towards Malek, her designated drink provider for the evening.

The music's volume made communication challenging, prompting Haya to lean in close to Malek's ear.

"I don't think I'm going to stay." Haya screams in Malek's ear.

"Don't be silly!" Malek shook his head dismissively, a wry smile on his face, as he handed Haya a drink. Haya nodded, but her fingers clutched her purse tightly, as if she were poised to leave at any given moment.

"Do you think he's going home with her?" she blurted out to Malek, downing her drink in a record ten seconds. Malek seemingly unfazed, raised an eyebrow.

"What?" he asked, lounging at the bar, immersed in the music and casually scanning the crowd, his attention momentarily diverted to a woman standing in front of him.

"Oh my God, he is going home with her!" Haya exclaimed without waiting for a response, her anxiety palpable. Malek sighed, his patience wearing thin.

"Will you stop this crazy behavior?" he implored, "and even if he does, what is the big deal? Also, can you please relax? We are not at a tea party!"

Malek and Kamal epitomized the archetype of masculine men who effortlessly attract female attention. Beirut seemed to be their playground, particularly since many young men their age had left the country in search of work abroad. When they were together, they would assess women with swift, sexual classifications. However, in the company of their female friends, their demeanor transformed from crude to gallant gentlemen, ready to provide support and companionship.

What Malek failed to grasp about Haya's behavior was her struggle to come to terms with the harsh realities of her own life. Unlike Laura, who had embraced her circumstances, Haya remained fixated on finding solace in the illusion of magic provided by the men she drew in, the elusive promise of future job opportunities, and the graceful façade she maintained in social settings.

She was forgetting that she lives in Lebanon.

Chapter 2: Stanley Kowalski

Beirut nightlife AD (After Destruction) is a toxic mixture of ferocious materialism and basic cravings. The basic cravings of Lebanese people have always been electricity, hot clean water, capable infrastructure and independent justice, because the education, healthcare and financial sectors were privately owned and had always been of exceptional high quality. That chasm between public and private services was always the source of the bloody enigma that tainted the country every now and then for years and years. Now however, since the country is officially a failed state, the only sector left functioning is the hospitality one and that has brought on an eclectic mix of stranded depravity that is somehow still enchanting to the outside world.

The Warehouse was the only lively haven left that was toiling beneath the surface, altering the radical decline of the civilization above, and so all the different creatures that were still available to party in the country, would harbor themselves after hours in an aesthetic depot to preserve whatever is left of human interaction.

As the night unfolded in a cacophony of laughter and clinking glasses, Malek stole a moment to observe Haya, who stood beside him, shamelessly yet delicately sipping on the leftovers of other people's drinks at the crowded bar. A couple of hours had passed since they arrived, and the lively atmosphere of the venue was dominated by a boisterous group of tourists whose language was completely unattainable to Haya.

The bustling locale teemed with life, resonating with the exuberant cheers of nearby tourists. Their enthusiasm seemed boundless, finding cause for celebration in even the most trivial of moments, such as the delivery of a fresh round of shots. Malek and Haya, amidst the whirlwind of festivities, exchanged a shared glance imbued with a mixture of amusement and exasperation. It was a silent acknowledgement of the vibrant chaos surrounding them, and a testament to the colorful jubilation of human experiences.

Swaying slightly, Haya leaned to Malek after he asked her if she was still waiting for something, "Well I couldn't leave without my cousin now, can I?" Her words were accompanied by a mischievous grin, echoing the dreadful thoughts he was concerned for her about.

Before he could say anything, he was abruptly interrupted by an unexpected splash, a doudou shot was carelessly launched from the neighboring exuberant group. Haya's borrowed shirt, that she managed to acquire from a nearby store without purchasing it, bore the brunt of the impact, officially rendering it ruined. The woman responsible for the unintentional assault apologized loudly, a mix of embarrassment and indifference evident in her tone. Malek couldn't help himself but break down in laughter, before he took his newly found date home and bid his friend adieu.

In the meantime, Kamal was dancing with Rena on the dance floor and only came to the bar to check if Malek still had any cash left for more alcohol.

"He just left!" Haya said idly when she saw Kamal looking around nervously.

"Huh! And why are you still here?" he asked carelessly

"Well, I guess alcohol does make you primitive after all." Haya answered the bar stools rather than Kamal himself.

"Excuse me?" he asked her curtly.

"Well, my cousin will not go for you, look at you!" She continued.

Kamal was practically glaring at her in that moment. Luckily for Haya, Rena joined them at the right time.

"Isn't my cousin the prettiest?" Rena asked swaying from side to side and then grabbing his arm tightly for balance.

"No!" Kamal said flatly. His crude response ultimately woke up the two women a tiny bit.

Rena took Kamal aside, "Do you not know my cousin at all?"

"I do he said!" casually running his hand through his hair and looking around at the place as it started emptying.

"Don't you know that you have to sugar coat everything and compliment her every now and then?"

"I do know that! In fact I do compliment her more than she deserves."

"So what was that about?"

"Demoiselle, I think your appearance will harness my affection tonight!"

Rena laughed and touched his muscular arm again, "But you didn't answer my question?"

"I am done with this conversation. Now would you like to accompany me home?" he asked her as he ran a finger under her cheekbone and down her neck.

Rena blushed, she couldn't let go of his hand even though she knew that if she left with him, he won't pursue her any further. "I'll go home with you if you tell me how I look in this moment?"

"Like a million dollars!" he laughed "Fresh."

It didn't sound like a compliment to Rena even though she knew the importance of fresh dollars to Lebanese people these days. Yet from someone like Kamal, she expected more enchantment, because in the few hours that she spent with him he seemed down-to-earth and sincere, and possessed a physical vigor that was evident in his carefree attitude towards life and even somehow with this strong dedication to his country and friends.

Rena ended up leaving home with Kamal who graciously offered to drop her shambling cousin home on the way.

"You know Rena, Kamal is the type of guy that bumps up one street and down another." Haya rambled from the back seat. Rena's eyes popped out from her head, she turned to face him as he was smiling and driving silently.

"Would you like me to drop you home too?" he asked her plainly before she managed to protest about her cousin's comment,

She was completely taken aback; he was making no effort to appease her anxious motivation about the whole situation.

"Actually yes" she replied sternly.

"Alright then!" he smiled at her gently.

"Would you mind unbuckling my shirt Kamal?" Haya asked from behind, "for some reason it is still wet and stuck everywhere."

"Sure!" he replied, he stopped the car on the side of the road and went down to help his friend with her sophisticated shirt of buttons and wraps. "It smells lemony." He smiled at her tenderly knowing that her ordeal is going to be costly.

When they finally arrived at Haya's house, Rena seemed to have changed her mind again, and when they said their good-byes, Rena remained in his car and asked him playfully;

"I think I might need a hot shower, Haya mentioned that hers is not working properly."

Kamal laughed heartily and asked "So I guess being a fashion marketer in London doesn't pay very well to be able to afford a hot shower in a hotel while on vacation?"

Rena, not one to back down, pulled up her hand to strike him, but he was too quick for her, grabbing her hand tightly and surprising her with a full kiss on her mouth. The unexpected gesture left her immensely thrilled.

"You know my cousin talks about you all the time." She confessed between laughs.

"Does she?" Kamal replied with a smile.

"Yes but you are nothing like how she describes you." Rena continued, completely betraying her cousin.

Kamal's interest piqued and he inquired "How does she describe me?"

"Well, a brutal libertine! If a distinctive character like you can be summarized eloquently!" Rena laughed at herself as soon as the words came out of her mouth.

"And what do you think?" he asked her with a smirk, as he parked his car under his house and went around to open the door for his guest.

"I can't think when you look at me." She replied softly.

"I know." he winked and led her up the stairs, their playful banter lingering in the air.

The next morning, Haya awoke with a throbbing headache, still clad in yesterday's clothes and smeared makeup; she had completely forgotten that Rena did not stay at her house last night.

As she made her way to the bathroom, she noticed her chestnut hair was a bit tousled, but oddly, that fact offered a small reprieve from self-criticism.

"She ended up staying at his place" she wrote frantically on her phone to Laura.

A few moments later she got a message;

"Yeah that was a given, LOL." Laura responded.

Haya's brown eyes widened in disbelief. Unable to contain herself, she dialed Laura's number and unleashed a torrent of words recounting the events of the previous evening. Interwoven with her narrative were constant references to the subjects of money and elusive hot water. Despite Laura's attempt to provide advice on Haya's habitual escapades, the conversation always concluded the same way, by Haya stating "I need to think!" before ending the call.

Chapter 3: Stella Kowalski

Mediocre leadership parades authority with the number of followers that have abandoned conventions of dignity as well as expectations of morality and become their worst selves, together. Since 2005, Lebanon experienced a wave of mediocre leadership that led to the eventual decline of a whole country. Total destruction began after the country abandoned the payment of a financial bond for the first time ever in its history in 2020. This is usually not a big deal since debt can be restructured, but the country was held up to default in one way or another and for reasons that remain a mystery until now.

Three years later the Lebanese developed a daily schedule that included; a few hours of natural sleep and then a couple more that are medicinally induced, an hour long of either breakfast, lunch or dinner, an hour to get to nearby places, because most people cannot afford public transportation while the rest have abandoned their cars and decided to take up walking or cycling, and finally endless hours of political debate in consecutive and ceaseless outings that seem to be funded by fairy godmothers. Quite the dystopian life, only the underlying forces that held up Lebanon for a financial decline, had another thing coming for them when they attempted to destroy the Lebanese individual.

Luckily the local tyrants that demanded obedience from their followers were finally defeated and were set apart as social pariahs, and there were no more social class struggles since everyone was suffering from financial distress. Laura was content enough about not dealing with the ideologies of the insane; she accepted the reality of her downturn and was looking for ways to protect her life from falling apart.

It was around 5 pm on a Saturday when Haya came knocking at Laura's house, she did not take a hint that Laura did not feel like having coffee and just wanted to sit alone in her peaceful bed with a good book.

"Hello Haya, how can I be of assistance today?" Laura joyfully mocked her friend.

Haya walked into the mediocre apartment with disappointment etched across her face.

"Am I overthinking this?" She finally asked her friend earnestly.

"Well yes, do you even want the guy? Seriously?" Laura probed, aware that Haya enjoyed attention from various men without harboring feelings for any in particular.

"Doesn't jealousy mean that I have feelings for the guy?" Haya asked, a note of confusion in her voice.

Laura thought about it for a moment, and then asked her "Are you still jealous now?"

"Yes!"

"Okay, so why don't you just tell him how you feel!"

"I insulted him multiple times yesterday, so I was almost sure that Rena would not go for him. But clearly she has no limits!" Haya began rambling on again.

At this point Laura began to believe that her friend might really like Kamal, but her behavior was too neurotic to take her seriously, so she chose to remain silent. She excused herself and headed to the kitchen to make coffee.

Oblivious to Laura's plans for solitude with a good book, Haya exuberantly called out as she lounged on her friend's comfortable green couch; "Oh we are not having coffee here!"

"Why? You were just saying this morning that you spent a lot of money yesterday."

"Oh, my dear, you take everything that I say way too seriously." Haya let out a small laugh, "Rena just messaged me to tell me to meet her for coffee, and you are coming with me."

"Oh no, oh no no no, please leave me out of this I beg you." Laura pleaded.

"Oh yes, and I am telling Malek to join too, after all, we all know who really influences Kamal," Haya exclaimed confidently.

Laura started towards her bedroom, "You are like my sister Laura, thanks a million for this. Can I have a shot of vodka please?"

"Help yourself!" Laura smiled faintly as she went to her room to put on a pair of flat black ankle boots over her skinny dark blue jeans.

"I really have to update those bottles in your bar!" Haya cried out, "It is in no condition to tolerate Lebanon these days."

AS THE TWO FRIENDS walked to the café, Haya noticed Laura's quiet demeanor and asked "Why are you so quiet?"

"I'm usually quiet when I have nothing to say" Laura replied.

"So how do I look?" Haya asked, completely ignoring her friend's answer

"You look good!" Laura answered while gazing up at the sky, pondering the prospect of snuggling up with that good book. She made a mental note to keep her phone on silent or pretend she wasn't at home the next time someone knocks on her door uninvited.

"I meant do I look Rena good?"

"Sure!" At this point, Laura feigned interest in her phone, almost dropping it when Haya cried out, "Malek, you are here! Thank God for you."

"They will be here in five minutes. Hello messy child!" Malek playfully ruffled Laura's burgundy hair as he updated Haya on the situation.

"I could use a drink!" Laura requested a menu from the waiter. She was actively avoiding her friends' chatter about the previous evening, and then suddenly she heard his clear radiant voice,

"I thought you would never come back to this café?" Kamal asked as he sat next to Laura after squeezing her shoulder.

"It has a convenient location for everyone these days!" she replied smoothly.

"It is for the woodland people, but it is the closest to Laura and Malek's house" Haya explained to Rena as the latter sat between her cousin and Kamal.

Rena's voice, sweet and soft, cut through the air as she expressed her fascination. Her eyes slowly drifted towards the interior of the cafe, more reminiscent of an outdated flower shop than a modern café. Laura, on the other hand, pondered how to effortlessly connect with Rena. The conventional icebreaker, "so what do you do," danced on the tip of her tongue, but she hesitated, not wanting to sound overprotective or overly intrigued about Kamal's ladies. Instead she chose a simpler question.

"Did you have lunch?" Laura inquired delicately.

Rena met her gaze, responding with a smile, "No, not yet."

The waiter returned with Laura's drink, leaning in towards her with a gracious smile that captured the attention of the entire table. Rena thought she can bring back the attention to herself, as the exotic stranger with a jest, "Now I know why you guys come here! It's because Laura gets free drinks!"

Ignoring the comment, Laura tuned into Malek's story about the woman he met the previous night. He described her as someone who works for an NGO and loves hiking, "She's very sporty!" He playfully winked at Kamal. In turn Kamal laughed and commented, "They all are these days!"

"What is that supposed to mean?" Rena asked Haya and Laura,

"It means that they have a lot of energy to spare." Laura replied curtly, she then turned to Kamal and gestured "Score" with her hand. "So where is that lady of yours Malek?" she smiled widely at him.

Seemingly annoyed by Kamal's comment and his friends' nonchalance about the subject, Rena sipped her drink silently. Haya attempted to break the awkwardness, nudged Malek and teased, "Yes, Malek! Where is she? She works at an NGO, so this means that she gets paid in fresh dollars."

Ignoring his friend's petty comment, Malek gulped down his bourbon.

Kamal looked at Haya and told her; "You remind me of my cat Ginger."

"Is he cute?" Rena asked a little hesitant,

"Very, in fact he is gorgeous and fluffy and cuddly." he continued, Rena was clearly not enjoying this, Laura was completely amused and Haya was beginning to unconsciously broaden her shoulders slowly.

Kamal then turned to Rena and held her hand "You see, he always plays with grasshoppers, yet even though he scratches them with his paw he still jumps away from them whenever they wriggle their thin legs. Eventually he kills them and some other times he might as well eat the creatures. To put it in psychological terms, just the way you like it Haya, Ginger's interaction with grasshoppers, from playful engagement to the eventual capture and consumption, is exactly what your jokes sound like."

Haya was not amused. Malek burst out laughing and Laura restrained her delirious composition.

Kamal continued, "Always remember Haya "A generous enemy is more helpful than a jealous friend.""

Rena, having listened to the story, felt a sense of relief, though a tinge of sympathy lingered for her cousin. To shift her focus, she absentmindedly scrolled through the menu on her phone before suddenly exclaiming, "Oh, there is potato pizza. I love that pie!"

"Seriously?" Laura asked, "I mean I know the menu is small but that is because the business has to ration the food so that they wouldn't be expensive for the locals with the ridiculous currency fluctuations, but there is prosciutto. Wouldn't that taste better with your wine?"

"Wow Laura, I can see you have taste!" Rena said condescendingly, "Are you a connoisseur?" she laughed a little.

Kamal jumped in, "Laura used to go out a lot, and enjoyed herself more than anyone can possibly imagine, always with the perfect orders, at the right spots!"

"You mean before the revolution?" Rena was insisting on the subject, sounding more juvenile by the minute,

"No, way before," Haya answered this time,

"I'm surprised she knows what prosciutto means." Rena whispered loudly to Haya. "I mean look at her outfit!"

Haya ignored her cousin and was checking something on her phone,

"Right! Well, that is my cue!" Laura excused herself,

"You always leave at the perfect time now." Malek said jokingly.

"I didn't mean to upset her." Rena whispered loudly to Kamal, not really meaning it.

"Not at all, I'm just allergic to this country, that's all." Laura smiled after overhearing the comment.

"Why? It is so much fun." Rena opened her arms wide while speaking.

"Yes for you! To me though, I find that the country is a lot like potato pizza, a pie full of cheap and abundant ingredients, that make it bland and yet somehow heavy!" Laura said with a quiver in her voice, and she left without saying goodbye to anyone.

Chapter 4: Belle Reve

Laura knew she was harsh with Rena, but she was heartbroken, this most certainly did not justify comparing a lady to a pizza pie, but then again the woman was getting on her nerves, and she wasn't exactly sure why. Sure she missed dressing up well, but she was relatively not in a glamorous mood anyway, with the country being what it is at the moment.

Laura slumped into her couch as soon as she got home and turned off her phone, she was in quite a state, she stared across her living room and slowly drifted into her thoughts, "Beirut ya Beirut." She said to herself, and was thinking about how when she was eighteen, she drew a picture of the city that she once loved so much.

Thirteen years ago, if a person was in a contest to choose the most civilized citizens of the world, it would have been preposterous not to say that it was the people of Beirut city. The Lebanese have always been multi-domiciled between the US, Europe and the Far East, automatically fluent in three languages, hospitable and generous by instinct, and always exquisitely dressed. At that time, they were conducting their lives in a physical setting so glamorous; nothing had yet been able to rival it.

When tourists came to Lebanon, they had to put in an effort to adjudicate finesse in everything, from conversations to fine dining. Basically the Lebanese were dubbed as the financial and entertainment geniuses. In a weekend, a tourist was able to dispute over Gebran, Hugo and Wilde, discuss Ottoman history, go wine-tasting in the Bekaa, splash around in the Mediterranean beach bars, feast like a Greek God, sing hymns at dinner with complete strangers, and witness furious political argument.

This was a subject that Laura and Haya argued about a lot during lockdown. Laura was still living in her Belle Reve version of Beirut, while to Haya the fact that there are always new places opening up meant that the outings will never stop. Laura did not care about the round of coffee shops with friends or cocktail sipping fiestas, she just dragged herself along so that she wouldn't be completely alone.

After what seemed like hours had passed, Laura woke up from her reverie due to the intense knocking at her door. She looked outside her window it was dark, she must have dozed off. She moved slowly to open her door, and there were Malek, Kamal, and Haya all staring at her angrily. She looked back at them calmly and said; "Guys! You really ought to get a life!"

"You left us at 5 pm; now it is 8 pm." Kamal told her strictly tapping his wrist as if there was a watch there, while pushing her aside so they could all go in.

"Did you lose your phone?" Malek asked concerned.

"No!" she exclaimed angrily, "Seriously you guys this is not healthy!"

"You are right!" Haya said, "But we all couldn't get a hold of you for hours. Why did you get so mad at my cousin?"

"Ok, I am going to be very mean now, but you are going to have to respect my decision; otherwise I doubt we will be able to remain friends." Laura said seriously. The three adults looked at each other and sat on the only couch in the small living room.

Laura started pacing in front of them "I am not your girlfriend or your wife or your daughter. In fact we are just friends, sometimes even acquaintances. I admit we became close because of lockdown, but guys I don't know anything about you before 2019, don't you find it weird?"

They all shook their heads.

"Don't you have other friends to worry about?" Laura asked with a small smile breaking on her face.

"We do!" Kamal said confidently, "But even if Ginger is irritable and gets erratic, I would like to know if he is ok!"

Haya looked at Kamal exasperated "Is Ginger the new sponsor of your conversations?"

He just laughed at her and turned to look at Laura, who seemed to be having an internal conflict with herself. It was stupid of Laura to turn off her phone without telling any of her friends that she reached the house or that she is sorry she left abruptly. Her mind was not with her, she didn't realize that she was kind of at fault.

"Alright then, now that we know that you are ok, I am going to see my date!" Malek said and kissed Laura on her cheek sweetly, "Please don't do that again!" he looked back at her as he shut the front door behind him.

"I like you more than my old friends." Haya smiled at her earnestly, "Call you tomorrow! I have this course to finish online!"

Laura and Kamal looked at her startled and then at each other. "I'm joking, I have a dinner." Haya burst out laughing. Kamal was the only one left on the couch, he was examining Laura quietly.

After a couple of minutes of pure silence Laura asked "Would you like something to drink?"

"Yes, a vodka please! Neat."

Laura came back with two glasses, and she sat next to him quietly, "Cheers." They clinked their glasses.

"You know for someone that is supposedly very smart, you can be incredibly stupid." Kamal said assertively.

"Enough! I am not up for your mood swings!"

"What mood swings?"

"You have mood swings in case you have no idea," Laura gestured to a book on a shelf above her television.

Kamal's eyes traced the spine of the book she pointed to, a playful grin dancing on his lips. "Please tell me you are joking?" he teased, turning to catch her gaze.

"Nope!" she joined him at her little shelf that was littered with books haphazardly. "In fact," she continued her voice laced with a mischievous tone, "I think that you may have more mood swings than me, a woman!"

As she took another sip of vodka, Kamal scanned the shelves, captivated by the disorder of her literary haven. She held books in both hands, attempting to convey her point, but her justification was lost in the charm of the moment.

"Sometimes you ask me something, and then you go silent for weeks," she lamented, her words punctuated by the clink of the glass meeting her lips. "And now you come with Malek and Haya, pretending that you care."

"I don't mean to. I just have things to do, I suppose," Kamal replied, hands on his waist, a hint of apology in his eyes.

"Please_" she began, but he interrupted gently, closing the distance between them.

"I'm sorry," Kamal whispered, the sincerity in his voice softening the room.

"Where is Rena?" Laura asked, her tone shifting.

"She went home to change! We are supposedly going out for dinner."

"Where to?"

"If I tell you, it is just going to upset you."

"Oh, for God's sake, not the Warehouse again." She laughed at him, a laugh with underlying softness that echoed through the room. "That is not dinner!"

He remained silent and she pressed on. "You know what makes me upset? When you used to come with me to the revolution, we made a promise that we will protect our city, our muse of fabulousness, to conserve this lovely place and life here, for its intellectual brilliance and for your beautiful ladies. You can invite her to your house for dinner; wouldn't it be more chic and romantic?"

"She is staying with me."

"Already!" Laura stepped back, annoyed, but Kamal didn't let her retreat.

"Yes. Listen, I don't usually mean to upset you." He said as he pulled her close to him.

Laura felt a little uncomfortable,

"Do I frighten you?" he asked, studying her eyes, searching for answers.

"I'm just very tired." She replied, avoiding his gaze.

He nodded silently, studying her movements, assessing her carefully.

"I love that you are still heartbroken." He told her softly.

"Aren't you?" she looked straight at him,

"Yes, but this is what it is about you.."

"It's not like it is easy to get over being constantly hurt for no reason for three years now," she confessed.

"I'm sorry," Kamal offered, his sincerity washing over her.

She shrugged, straining for nonchalance, "I suppose I'm not the only one, and it is hardly your fault."

"It's our destiny." He whispered with a small laugh, drawing back her attention.

She looked up at him and realized his nose was a mere millimeter away. In an impulsive moment she leaned into him, capturing his lips in a kiss. In that instant, it felt like he was her destiny, and who was she to argue with her fate, having changed so many times in the course of three years. Besides, there was truth or a murky story to back up this impulsiveness, and in the imagination of a romantic, the more vodka infused, the murkier is the moment.

Chapter 5: Harold Mitchell

Ten years pre-revolution; business moguls, warlords, infamous architects and terrorists had to keep up standards. They were cool, young at heart and so dazzlingly well put together, that they had an ethereal glow that mesmerized the world. It was perfectly normal to go into an internationally renowned bar in downtown Beirut and find a politician drinking on the bar alone, before heading back home after a long day during the week. Malek and Kamal were these heartbreakingly likable, erudite, cultivated people that drank and wenched together. Even though they came from different schools of thought, they both knew they were too wonderful as human beings to fight each other.

After the revolution, and despite Kamal's great sense of disappointment in Malek, because the latter did not take part in the great rebellion, he knew he needed Malek to come back from his self-purgatory and embrace a little hedonism while their world crumbles. To Kamal, he had taken enough beatings in the protests on multiple occasions to give up on democracy, transparent government, cultural openness, fierce hard work and rule of law. There was no visible way for him to get there from here or at least a way that involves a painless passage for the time being. And so like most of the Lebanese that decided to remain in the country, he was stuck with his best friend in a capsule of time where there was no way of looking back, no stable present and a dim future. What they did maintain to keep up though were the standards.

Malek and Kamal found themselves in the midst of a casual afternoon, the aroma of chicken shawarma filing the air as they stood at a curbside snack shop.

What had happened in their lives over a course of a very short time, left them both bewildered and amused, they found themselves tackling unprecedented situations with a blend of resilience and humor, often exchanging playful banter to make sense of it all. Their sanctuary, their haven of shared laughter and light-hearted musings, was none other than the cozy confines of their beloved snack shop. Here amidst the comforting aroma of fresh savory sandwiches, they found solace in each other's company, exchanging stories of their intimate adventures with a touch of whimsy and a dash of sarcasm.

"Are you taking Rena out tonight?" Malek asked Kamal after biting into his succulent sandwich.

"Yeah!" Kamal replied after swallowing his bite, a flicker of excitement in his eyes as he looked at his sandwich.

"Oh great, I'm thinking of hanging out with Laura tonight." Malek shared casually, taking another bite of his sandwich.

Kamal was caught slightly off guard, coughed a little, pretending he had something stuck in his throat. "What are you planning on doing?" he asked, trying to sound nonchalant.

"I'm going over to her place. What are you planning with Rena?" Malek inquired, leaning against the snack shop's counter.

"I don't know, The Roof bar, then maybe my place," Kamal replied, his expression suddenly fading in excitement.

"Cool!" Malek nodded in approval, savoring the flavor of his heavenly lunch.

There was something to Middle Eastern food that offered a way for people to perpetuate their creation. It wasn't just an everyday event, there was something deeper. Usually when food is abundant and people are preoccupied with other distractions, nobody thinks of its value. However, when people are hungry they realize its sustenance for life. To a hungry person, a stale piece of bread may taste better than a banquet in times of plenty. A shawarma sandwich however defies the two extremes in being just like a Lebanese, a constant delight that is always sought out to be devoured.

The conversation took a turn as Kamal shifted the focus. "How's your mother doing? He asked, showing genuine concern.

"Same old, needs a lot of attention. In fact, I need to go look for her medicine now, she's running out." Malek shared, a touch of responsibility in his voice.

"Need help looking?" Kamal offered. The glow of the sun cast a warm ambiance as they continued their conversation while the day unfolded with the promise of plans and the comfort of friendship.

"Really? Don't you have things to do, like get ready for your date?" Malek poked fun at his mate, and feeling a little better that he wasn't going to be alone in his quest.

"Nah, I'm already trimmed." Kamal replied jokingly and rubbed his friend's shoulder.

To find certain medications in Beirut was truly an arduous business, it took no less than a couple of hours, and if the medicine is found, it was excruciatingly expensive. In fact, the country would have been the perfect case study for Murray Rothbard, the leading theoretician of anarcho-capitalism. Just as he writes in his articles; the case of Lebanon became a state that seized to exist and all its provisions, including education, healthcare, environmental protection and transport infrastructure, were supplied through NGOs. According to Rothbard, this system would not only lead to a better-functioning economy, but was also morally correct. Well maybe he should have asked the Lebanese standing in queues at bakeries, gas stations and pharmacies, if the experience felt morally dignified.

Taking the Rothbard example a step forward, he believed that governments financed themselves through taxes which people paid involuntarily, and competition lowers prices. Indeed he was right for the most part, women in Lebanon started competing ferociously for sugar daddies to pay for their lifestyles and there was no one better than Malek and Kamal at providing that service in an incredibly low cost environment.

"The girl from the Warehouse is calling me?" Malek looked at his phone as it vibrated silently.

"Great, take her out then tonight." Kamal urged him. "Lets's go out all together!"

"No I don't feel like it, I want to be with Laura."

"Yes but you are not going to have fun with Laura." Kamal ran his hand through his coal-black hair, looking at the ground, trying to hide his anxiousness.

"True, but Laura doesn't tease me in different languages because she knows I won't understand, or try to belittle my barbell activities just because they do not fit her world!"

"She's not a headache!" Kamal continued

"Exactly, I can be clumsy and sweaty and she will laugh." Malek explained.

Kamal sighed trying to hide his indignation, he knew there was nothing going on between his two friends and nothing ever will, but it was too damn well annoying.

Malek and Kamal were about forty years of age, and the very mould of chivalry as gentlemen could ever be. Debonair and dainty, they reflected the values their Lebanese mothers enforced in their children. Whoever called Lebanon the Switzerland of the Middle East knew the values that Lebanese mothers enforced in their children and continued to reinforce until their deaths; that meant that they had to dress up properly, be clean, have manners, be polite and kind to others, as well as respect and care for each other. Laura regarded Malek and Kamal as feat and trim as a person could possibly be, while Haya being very sensible of the advantages their person brings to her considered their friendship after a few small favors.

It was around 6pm when Malek got to Laura's house with a bottle of gin and a couple of tonic cans.

Laura opened the door, her hair was tied up in a bun and she was wearing a dark blue cotton dress with long sleeves, it reached her ankles but highlighted her slim shape very stylishly.

"Hello gorgeous!"

"Malek! I love you" she exclaimed while hugging him.

She led him to her open kitchen and they sat on the high stools of her kitchen table as they fixed their drinks while rambling on about their day. She had ordered pizza but asked for them to be delivered at around 8pm. Her table was laid with white linen and beeswax candles, Malek was surprised she had ordered pizza because there were so many bread sticks and an open recipe book for "Midnight Chicken" by Ella Risbridger. He started reading out loud;

"Chicken, garlic, chili, rosemary, thyme, mustard, ginger, honey and lemon."

"So how's your new girlfriend?" she asked him teasingly.

"I have no idea!" he laughed "This recipe seems delicious and it's making me hungry!"

"It is, and should be drank with a Martini but I'm not going to cook for you and I don't have Martini." She replied assertively yet sweetly and then asked him; "Didn't she ask about her chivalric hero?"

"I'm only her hero when it comes to alcohol supply and Asian meals!" he joked, but then quickly frowned since he realized how duping it was of the girl he was currently dating to extract things from him that were so trivial. Then he said as he was turning the pages of the cookbook, "Oh my, my mouth is watering, rib-eye seared with butter."

"I'm going to get the pizza now, you are breaking my heart," she texted the pizza place on her phone and told Malek" don't feel so glum about that girl, you both shared a mutual need." She winked at him.

"You are absolutely right! How is that going for you?" he teased her, "What is up with your cookbooks, Gnudi, Bagna cauda. They are killing me." They both laughed as he scanned her tiny shelf under her kitchen table that had a couple of recipe books.

"Mmmm not sure I haven't been caught in that snare yet!" she explained, in that moment the doorbell rang, "Oh this must be the pizza! Your stomach will soon be saved!" she chuckled to herself.

Laura ran to open the door and was startled to see Kamal and Rena standing there.

"Heyy guys!" Laura told them with genuine surprise.

Malek did not have the same friendly approach, in fact he looked angry. "What are you doing here?" he glared at his friend.

"We thought we would crash your party since I ran out of ideas of where to take Rena." Kamal explained to his two friends who seemed to have frozen in their place.

"We brought you Gin, Kamal said it's your favorite." Rena told Laura with a smile.

The four friends sat around the dimly lit kitchen table, the bits and pieces of their pizza feast scattered before them, the silence hanging thick in the air. Laura, sensing the need to break that deafening silence proposed a game. The game was called "This or That". They were to ask the person sitting to their right two random questions, no need for complexity or deep contemplation, and the respondent had to choose one of the options presented.

Laura initiated the game by turning to Malek. "Beirut or Tripoli?" she asked him. Without much hesitation he replied "Tripoli!" The game was set in motion.

Malek, in turn, dedicated his question to Rena. "Long dress or short dress?" he inquired. Rena, initially considering the context, found herself corrected by Laura. "Nope! Just pick one." Laura interjected. Rena, seeking guidance from Kamal, received no help, and so finally settled on "Short!" Kamal, amused by the turn of events, clinked his glass with hers.

Now it was Rena's turn to ask Kamal. "London or Beirut?" Kamal, pretending to be brimming with enthusiasm, exclaimed loudly for the purpose of shock and entertainment "Beirut!" His fervent response elicited laughter from the group, it was evident the game was doing its job.

With everyone in good spirits, Kamal turned to Laura for his question. "Pizza or burger?" he asked with an impish grin, ready to keep the lighthearted momentum of the game going.

"Cheese burger!" she answered cheekily,

"So why did you get us pizza then?" he asked her brazenly,

"You weren't even invited!" Malek interrupted him.

"Yes, but we brought her Gin." Rena added this small detail as if it's a bargaining chip for making up for the fact of showing up uninvited.

"Yes, thank you Rena." Laura laughed a little as she walked towards her bar and opened up a cupboard that was full of different kinds of gin,

"Here taste this!" Laura told Rena, as she handed her a glass of Japanese gin that Laura simply loved.

"Oh yum what is it?"

"What we are drinking, but neat."

"It tastes better neat!" Rena exclaimed excitedly.

"I know! Enjoy!"

Chapter 6: Doomsday Book

Lebanon post-2020 was shoved back to a lifestyle that existed more than a hundred years ago, with Lebanese people's deposits locked up in banks under an unlawful capital control regulatory framework; the Lebanese were not able to venture near or far. Their lives were spent sowing herbs from dismal pots grown on the roof of buildings or balconies, then heaving groceries along uneven roads because it was too expensive to use any form of transportation and, at night, baths were taken after heating water on gas stoves, and if that was too costly, then they would literally heat water on open fires in neighborhoods that were plagued with prolonged and complete blackouts. Prayers were recited hourly, because any form of a lifestyle glow ultimately shrank to a candle shining through a kitchen window.

The Lebanese on October 16, 2019 were unlikely candidates for such a life. They never thought that their life would shrink to that enclosed world of rituals which was all about biding ones time. Even though Covid-19 lockdowns were full proof that sometimes life is halted for no reason at all and all a person can ever do is pause. The unearthly bliss to which all the strands of a person's subsequent happiness are tied, became obsolete in a Lebanese person's life because of the refusal to accept ones reality, and even after the August 4 explosion, which was tragic on every possible level imaginable and unimaginable, they were unable to propel themselves from materialistic indulgences.

Up until today, the air of anguish has not yet settled in Beirut, and yet, there is a form a mundane callousness that is truly unexplainable. Usually a tragedy can instill, for all its pain, a determination, an ambition, a premature adulthood that is often a precursor to success. But the Lebanese person's spiritual progeny post-2020 is content to cultivate an unchanging world and royally bent on seeking validation from materialistic things rather than traverse to minds that can soar into ideas and abstraction.

After a couple of hours of playing the game and sharing stories at key intervals and with an air thick with swirling smoke and laughter, Rena sensed a twinge of guilt tugging at her conscience. Despite the exhilarating company she was in, Rena couldn't shake the feeling that she should reach out to Haya. It struck her suddenly that Haya's friends who were perhaps preoccupied by the excitement of the moment had neglected to extend the invitation, and so she quickly called her cousin to rectify the oversight and ensure that Haya felt included and valued.

Haya showed up at Laura's building half an hour later. The woman on the ground floor peeped her head as she saw Haya rushing up the stairs;

"Do you have a problem with someone outside?" The little old woman asked,

"Excuse me?" Haya asked her surprised that there was someone actually living in this place. A radio call-in program blared from just behind the old lady, competing with a TV at the far end of the tiny apartment.

"I am Norma. I own this building." The old woman smiled up at Haya.

"Haya! Laura's friend. Up on the third floor." She smiled widely at the little old woman.

"There's a lot of noise coming from above or is it from outside?" Norma asked concerned. She was wearing a blue twinset that was piling at her hips, even though it was past her bedtime.

"Do you live alone here?" Haya asked her, gesturing to the noise coming from the tiny apartment and hoping the old lady would realize that the noise she is concerned about is actually coming from her own apartment.

"Yes, and you shouldn't walk in this neighborhood alone, pretty girl like you, at this hour!"

Haya nodded and smiled. Laura lived at the far end of a neighborhood that used to be bustling with a high end lifestyle and is as removed from gangland warfare as one could possibly imagine, but there was nothing to be gained to contradict this poor old woman's worldview because, in Lebanon after the sun sets, there is no more light, and when there is no more light then there is no more safety.

"I HAVE COME TO A FEW conclusions!" Haya stammered angrily at her friends as soon as she reached Laura's apartment, "you guys are either actively ignoring me, or you can't afford my outings anymore?"

Kamal looked straight at her and said "Haya! You are hardly a symbol of mystery let alone intriguing to the imagination. However, you most certainly are a cloudburst within our society that has fallen from absolutely nowhere!"

Haya had tears in her eyes, and was turning to leave before Laura came and hugged her, "Forgive him please Haya, he is drunk and clearly angry about something." Laura threw him an ugly look.

Rena told Kamal, "I wonder what on earth happened to you in this life that made you this bitter?"

They all turned at once and stared at Rena since clearly not only did she sound out of touch with reality, but under what circumstances, did she assume that the Lebanese in general are not angry.

Malek told them after a few minutes of silence "We've all had a lot to drink guys, let it go. And Kamal enough with poetry for the mad people!"

With that clearance from Malek, it was Haya's turn to explode "Since I am clearly the only one sober here, I would like to clarify something to Kamal." She turned towards Kamal and approached him slowly; "I have always wondered where you grew up?"

"That is not a clarification!" Laura Laughed,

Haya chuckled with Laura and then continued; "You see my darling Laura, a person's adult life is always shaped by his childhood. The tender, early years of raw perception usually lay the foundation of a mature mind." Haya gave Laura the white wine bottle she had brought her "Would you mind?" unable to manage the corkscrew Laura had given her.

"Ah yes, the therapist is at work now." Kamal joked. "Have a drink, I beg you!"

Haya took a glass and drank it down with one gulp, feeling proud she finally got to him.

"Kamal is driven by principles that were transformed into brilliant pieces of articles, which I'm sure you have even read Rena!" Malek explained to the ladies.

"You are a journalist?" Rena asked Kamal, wondering why she just found out about his occupation after having lived with him for a couple of days now.

Kamal grinned at her playfully, his dark eyes sparkling with a hint of lightheartedness. "A politician!" he declared, punctuating his words with a wink in Rena's direction. "And tonight, my dear, I'll start by transforming the country with you by me side." With a gallant gesture, he extended his elbow towards her, inviting her to join him on his grand endeavor.

Filled with a mix of excitement and intrigue, Rena eagerly accepted Kamal's invitation, her heart racing with anticipation for the passion that lay ahead. Together they departed without so much as a farewell to the others that were present.

Haya was catching up with the rest by drinking straight from the bottle,

"Malek? Are you finding your mother's medications?" She asked him earnestly.

"What I can find, minus the shame factor." he replied smiling wryly at his glass,

"Cheers to the shame factor." Laura exclaimed,

They clinked their glasses.

"I wonder what dignity feels like?" Haya asked herself mostly, in a sad tone.

Haya had always explained to her friends that brushes with death had a clarifying effect on the mind, values came into stark relief and decisions became simple and easy. However she did not practice what she preached, her recovery from the explosion had been plagued with drowsiness and indecision. Nothing had come into focus except the generous fellow-feeling that she felt when around Laura, Kamal and Malek. The others were just relieved to be alive, and they were cheerful enough, because the circumstances of the country didn't allow them to make any decisions about their future lives, and so they lived in the present.

Doing things was Haya's way. Always impatient, opportunistic and yet very slow to be thoughtfully pragmatic, nonetheless she just got on with whatever was going on. Just like how the whole world was offering Lebanon help because the explosion clarified and intensified the feelings of those watching the doomsday event, Haya was not able to understand that for now a fellowship was all she can get as well as certainty in a lie in wait mode for this hard time to pass.

Haya stood outside on Laura's tiny balcony that was overflowing with plants, the moonlight was bouncing off the windowed room. The scene was quiet and in the hush Haya was hard pressed to ask her friends if they were pro or con Rena and Kamal's relationship. Instead she just popped her head inside the apartment and asked Laura if this area is considered uptown or downtown.

Laura was unsure if her friend intended that as a slight, so she answered her thoughtfully "does it matter these days?" and she winked at Malek.

Haya was getting more anxious and there was no point in opening up the conversation she really wanted to get into now. Once something was fixed in the firmament as an object to be discussed, there was no point in being for or against it especially if it had reached a status that was already beyond the person debating it.

After a couple of drinks Haya stared out at the darkness in front of her and there was something sparkling about it, mordant and wistful, self-lacerating and romantic. She felt like she was watching her life with her friends from the grave, and maybe because she had nothing left to lose, there was an inimitable freedom that allows a person to live their life precisely as they wished.

There was no more room for a story that is conventional and hovers at the edges of love triangles and moneyed classes. Despite her resolute will to marry with the ambition to rise in society and have people mention her at any rate, this narrative was long gone in Lebanon. She wondered if her cousin would pass up the chance to marry Kamal and she ends up being his honorable wife instead, taking up the family mentorship or political life, therefore being catapulted to the center of social gossip in a swift manner. Then again what if her cousin does end up marrying Kamal and then she begins an affair with him, and try, not so hard really, to keep it hidden from Rena, but then somehow everyone would find out, and with the danger of discovery she is drawn even closer to Kamal.

As she stood contemplating the different scenarios with the aid of the immense darkness around her she felt a certain comfort in the radical notion that humans should be allowed to do anything humans naturally do, after all whatever ends up happening is meant to happen, with a special reverence for "Love".

Chapter 7: Le Risque Aleatoire

Nobody likes routine, and usually therapists suggest to patients ridden with indifference to embrace dislocation from their everyday lives in order to build confidence and reframe their priorities through novel experiences. But routine in Lebanon would do everyone good, since nothing but random events have been occurring, and no they weren't just incalculable risks, the events actually happened! The result of the extreme events led to the same results of what routine usually does to people living in well ordered environments; dulling people's sense of curiosity, purpose and wonder, leaving them looking back on their lives with regret.

For the Lebanese who had spent most of their lives deliberately choosing to live a routine life, and especially during the period after the war which lasted around thirty years almost, there was nothing gratifying in surrendering to a failed economy after four years of zero accountability for exceptional corruption. There was no acceptance of the situation, but there was also no will to do anything about it, especially three years on from the ultimate demise. For Laura though, she was a lot like the city of Beirut. She had accepted defeat, and was ok with the idea of floating with the wind, regardless of where that may take her. She got punched in the face with economic reality and was not willing to experience another sort of beating.

On the contrary Haya had honed her skills to take advantage of the survival mode, much like the Lebanese people in general, and because of the rack and ruin in their prime, anything can and should be done for the sake of creating a world that is calm and exemplary.

However, when radical events shift a person's life in unforeseen directions, usually skills should be honed vertically instead of horizontally. For the Lebanese and especially Haya, the skills were developed horizontally which led to extending the nightmare. Instead of changing altitude, and succumbing to ones faith of simplicity, Haya caught the same wind that led to Lebanon's financial devastation, the "Fake it until you make it" approach.

Beirut city knew what was holding it back; not everyone flourished during its pro-democracy movement, which led to a lot of resentment from people who wanted to live in a westernized country but at the same time despised the people who were living exquisitely well, and so they aligned themselves with the extremist political factions in the country and led a very delicate dance around the minefields of politics that ultimately led to stalemate and eventually imploded the country.

Laura asked Haya if she would join her for a walk on Corniche Beirut, there was something she wanted to tell her friend about for a while now, but because of their nascent yet somehow close relationship, she had been hesitant. As the two walked next to the palm trees that were lined on the waterfront esplanade, taking in the views of the summits of Mount Lebanon and breathing in the smell of the Mediterranean sea, Haya was the first to speak, as their conversation drifted between the waves and the complexities of human relationships;

"I admire you so much, you know that right?"

Laura was astounded, she didn't like being complimented and didn't enjoy flattery, there was always something behind that, and so she changed her mind from wanting to discuss the topic with her, and replied sheepishly, "Thank you!" she looked down at her four year old white trainers that were still fine and even looked good on the grey cement, and lamented the moment she asked for that walk.

Haya, seemingly oblivious to Laura's polite expression of gratitude, continued; "The way you drop people from your life, it's incredible, it's like dropping ballast!"

Laura squinted her eyes as she looked out at the calm sea, what on earth was she thinking, attempting to discuss Kamal with a woman she was beginning to label as selfish.

"So how do you stay calm?" Haya asked nervously.

"Arent you the psychologist?" Laura asked her nervously,

"Sure, but I am smart enough to understand my limitations."

"Goodness."

"Tell me, because I'm not you, I can't live alone or be alone."

"Well, it's as you said I drop ballast, only I do this after giving people a lot of chances."

"How many chances?" Haya insisted on apprehending the context.

"It's not about the number of chances but the amount of time in which the same issue is still bothering me from that person. Or something of the sort!" Laura laughed at herself.

"So you basically know what upsets you?"

"Of course! Don't you?"

"No," Haya looked down at her brand new light gray trainers in dismay, "I have no idea what holds me back!"

"What?" Laura was genuinely shocked, "How is that possible? You are thirty eight."

"I mean I know some things, but I'm not resolute about every aspect of my life, like you!" Haya beamed at Laura, making the latter feel uncomfortable again.

Laura inhaled through her nose and exhaled an enormous amount of breath through her mouth as she looked out at the sea, a typical ujjayi breathing followed to get through this afternoon peacefully. "You can always start by shedding everything that annoys you, from spending habits to physical exercises to meaningful relationships."

"I guess Kamal holds me back!" Haya blurted out honestly,

Laura's heart dropped suddenly, but she said nothing.

Haya continued "He likes you."

"He likes you too."

"No, no he likes YOU!" Haya poked her friend's shoulder with her finger lightly.

Laura laughed and tried to shrug it off "he likes your cousin Rena, stop flattering me. I don't like it!"

"He doesn't give a shit about my cousin, even she knows that."

Laura was starting to feel a little irritated, where was all this coming from she wondered to herself.

"He thinks you are like a pioneer." Haya continued.

"Ahh you mean, he admires me?" Laura asked her friend cautiously.

"Yes which means he likes you"

"No it just means because we worked in similar fields and we have a lot in common, so we get along well. That is it." Laura explained.

Haya looked up at the sky and then at her friend, "You are absolutely right. Its intellectual, ouf my God what a relief, it was annoying me so much. I am so glad it is out in the open and we are talking about this."

"Why was it annoying you so much?" Laura asked, trying to hide her agitation.

"I guess because we all seek conclusions from what we feel in the moment when we ask the questions, instead of actually weighing the question itself."

"Wow! Now that was theoretical." Laura laughed.

"It's Lebanon, it has become too narrow." Haya told her friend confidently, "attached to dismal habits, radical dogmas and negative beliefs."

"I know! That is why we have to keep an open mind." Laura reassured her friend.

"So, are you going to help me break up Kamal and Rena?" Haya asked excitedly.

"No, you psycho!" Laura grabbed her friend's hand and dragged her home, "Let's see what Malek is up to?"

Haya wanted to take pleasure whenever the opportunity presented itself. Laura on the other hand had always connected sex with love and love with destiny, and so literal was her interpretation that she failed to realize that people could be attractive because of their fleeting presence. She was unconsciously looking at Haya as they walked back to their apartments, and was wondering how her friend spent her life kissing men on the basis of an elaborate network of predestination. Haya tried to explain to Laura on multiple occasions how there was a certain instinctive satisfaction in kissing men on the slimmest of pretexts.

"Haya you are a passionate creator!" Laura exclaimed as she hung up the call with Malek. She had successfully convinced him to join them at the beach next to the esplanade.

The beach, the chance to sit peacefully on the rocks; were things the four friends all shared and loved. The incredible warming of the current weeks was striking anxiety but it also reminded them of how valuable a breeze is, how remarkable a deep-blue winter day can be and how precious the cool breeze that brushed in when night falls. How stunning Beirut was in its natural form, it has remained stirringly beautiful and that beauty must be one of the things that moves every Lebanese that lives abroad to come back home one day.

The October 17, 2019 revolution was the beginning of troubling times for the Lebanese people, it has dominated Lebanese politics for three years now, with many people losing their livelihoods and eyesight in the process. Reflecting on Lebanon's turbulent history, one might argue that such adversities were not entirely foreign, particularly amidst the fifteen-year war that once ravaged the country. However, following three decades of relative tranquility, despite occasional bomb blasts and looming threats during this purported "peaceful" era, the Lebanese had grown accustomed to disruptions in their daily routines.

So, one might wonder, how dire could these past three years truly be? Unlike the war-torn era marked by bomb scares and violent explosions, the calamity that ensued after the August 4 explosion overshadowed all else, leading to the absence of Lebanese militias patrolling the streets, which that in itself ought to be relieving.

However, in the midst of this upheaval, Beirut society was blessed with short periods of levity, from playful antics to nonsensical banter that had become emblematic of everyday life. Despite the looming specter of adversity, Laura found solace in the familiarity of her tight-knit circle of friends, where irreverent humor and a sense of camaraderie flourished against a backdrop of unfathomable cruelty.

While thoughts of fleeing Beirut often occupied her mind, she also found comfort in the sanctuary of home, her country, where laughter served as a fleeting refuge from the harsh realities of the outside world.

Chapter 8 Tragic Confrontations

The beauty of human beings lies in their struggle to stay alive. As adolescents, they tend to have a symmetrical spirit within an upright posture, as well as gleaming eyes that suggest relatively minimal scars. All of a sudden, a revolution happens promising the most preferable lifestyle to be sought for, desired and yearned for, only to be politically crushed. A pandemic overtakes the globe, a financial crisis develops and a city blows up. These events tend to make a human being's spirit asymmetrical and turn proper adolescents into elderly figures in as little as three years.

After the Beirut explosion, the United Nations appealed for $344.5 million in emergency funds to last until November 2020 in addition to the donor conference that was co-hosted by France and the UN just days after the blast, but by early September only 16.3% of the funds had been received. Of the total pledges, $84.5 million was meant for securing and repairing shelter, but only $1.9 million had been dispersed. Despite Covid-19 highlighting that our wellbeing, health and dignity are all bound up in each other and the key to social improvement and economic expansion is cooperation, in addition to the multiple global initiatives that promoted toolkits during lockdown to educate and empower people to build their own mutual aid networks throughout their buildings, blocks, neighborhoods and cities, emphasizing a focus on solidarity instead of charity; the Lebanese people gave the mutual aid projects to the NGOs that became a form of political participation in which some political parties took responsibility of certain groups of people, instead of caring for one another and changing political conditions as a whole.

The lack of solidarity between the Lebanese themselves allowed room for expatriates and foreigners to engage in ongoing charity; and so for three years Lebanon has been in crisis, in isolation and in silent protest.

There is an old saying that says "if you are not paying for some product or service, then you are the product or service," basically most of the Lebanese became the product of international NGOs who in turn were selling their attention and behavior to the countries that they reported to.

Rena enrolled herself in an NGO through an online platform, thinking she could take her mind off of Kamal's recent nonchalant attitude by doing something useful, so she started working as a researcher for an English NGO that deals with young adults struggling with the horrifying acts and events that had occurred in their relatively short lives. The office of the NGO was a small tent next to a night club that was named after a porn movie, the nightclub was a gleam in 2009 yet that was a whole other world altogether. When Rena mentioned where her new job was going to be, Kamal couldn't help but comment about the porn movie and Beirut's glorious days.

At the NGO she found herself dealing with unprecedented and multifaceted crisis, and mentioned casually to one of the volunteers that this was too dark for her to handle. The volunteer scoffed at her and gave her the small pamphlet of the NGO's mission to read. It said: "The economic and financial downturn, which commenced in October 2019, evolved into a relentless ordeal, compounded by the dual blows of the Covid-19 and the catastrophic explosion at the Port of Beirut in August 2020. Among these crises, the economic downturn stands out as the most pervasive and enduring, casting a shadow of despair over the nation. According to the Spring 2021 Lebanon Economic Monitor, this economic and financial debacle stands among the most severe globally since the mid-nineteenth century. The once robust nominal GDP, which neared $52 billion in 2019, now languishes at an estimated $23.1 billion in 2021. The prolonged economic contraction has inflicted a significant toll on disposable income, resulting in a staggering 36.5% drop in GDP per capita between 2019 and 2021."

Rena breathed heavily, this was too intense, and she drank a glass of water before she read on: "The World Bank, acknowledging the severity of Lebanon's economic plight, reclassified the country in July 2022, downgrading its status from upper-middle income to lower-middle income. This stark downgrade is a poignant reflection of the nation's economic freefall, a descent typically associated with times of conflict or war. Lebanon once a beacon of prosperity now stands at a crossroads, struggling with the profound implications of a crisis that transcends economic dimensions and permeates the very fabric of its society."

Rena quickly realized that there was going to be some sort of improvisation on her part when dealing with the young adults, it was as real as the situation can get, and what Rena thought would be a time to pass was quickly turning into a huge responsibility, so she decided to ask for something that has to do with a particular age group of the survivors of the explosion since there ought to be a bit of lightness and gag in this slight surreality.

Her first task was to interview a couple that had gotten married a few months before the revolution in 2019 and now have moved in with the lady's parents because their house was blasted during the explosion and they did not receive any help from any NGO to renovate their home, while at the same time they were not able to access their own money from the bank to repair it.

Rena wore blue tight jeans, a grey sweatshirt from Kamal and white sneakers for her first interview, she looked natural and light, and she was feeling good about her day ahead.

She only knew that the couple was a bit younger than her and that was a relief to her, but she did not think for a second that she would find them smiling and laughing together, she knew from her cousin that there was a bit of fun but not that much, and so when she encountered their cheerful disposition she felt a little jealous because she wasn't even that content with her own life. After a brief conversation while writing down their names and credentials, she asked them;

"Do you regret your time here in Lebanon the past three years?"

The couple replied that they are certainly not eager to repeat the experience.

"Can you tell me more about your experience after the August 4, explosion?"

The guy who was called Elias began "Well, May and I had to move to her parents' house after the explosion, but when I first went to check our home a few weeks later, the place felt different, and I immediately knew that our spirit in that house was gone."

Rena tried not to laugh, and when May saw her cover her mouth she was indignant so she asked Rena; "Imagine going inside your home where the bed has been made but is littered with debris, the kitchen counters covered in rubble, but there is a note on a broken desk that is torn from a page of one of your notebooks that says that some people will come and clean in the next few days. How would you feel?"

Rena answered her; "Well thankful to be alive, and that there are people willing to come and help me!"

May asked her; "So you wouldn't mind that people went through your things?"

"I do mind-" Rena began,

"So you wouldn't feel violated?" May asked again,

"I'm just trying to help!" Rena snapped at the couple,

"Don't you scribble your ideas in notebooks or have photos saved on USBs in your house?" Elias asked her, ignoring her reaction.

"Of course!" she replied curtly realizing her limitations,

"And what do you think is the spirit of a home?" May asked her.

Rena was quiet and started scribbling in her own notebook trying to avoid their gaze.

May's questions were brief and to the point, and it was clear to them that Rena was not in touch with their reality, just like all the NGOs that were gung ho in the aesthetics of the tragedy, while completely neglecting the human spirit.

"Does it bother you Elias to live with May's parents?" Rena asked, thinking this was what they were talking about.

"Well her parents are comfortable enough that we never felt the pressure of moving."

"And how have you been spending your time?" Rena asked robotically,

"Volunteering!" The couple replied as they smiled at each other.

Rena was a little surprised at their response and given what she had read at the NGO the previous day, "I guess it's like the new gap-year trend? Like backpacking though Europe used to be?"

"No, it is like living in a failed state, and helping in every possible way you can so that your society doesn't fail." Maya explained to her directly.

"And how would you describe this experience?" Rena asked them as she scrolled through the interview questions on her pad,

"The most difficult and the most rewarding thing we've ever done." The couple smiled at each other again.

"Would you think this passion is because of a privileged background?" Rena was now completely aggravated by their cheerfulness.

"Her parents are well off, mine are not, but we both discovered a passion within ourselves to help other people." Elias answered her.

"Many people will find it difficult to understand." Rena explained to them.

"We know that!" Elias said, "We feel sorry for them, because they are stuck in a small world, too scared to confront the great problems of our time."

"The explosion clearly awoke a lot of passion!" Rena expressed a little wisdom.

At this point there was nothing left to be discussed, and Rena smiled at them thinking she had aced her job, only for the lady with chestnut hair and wide brown eyes to put her hand on the file Rena was holding and say;

"If someone would give me the chance to rewind time and asked me if I can choose to be living here or abroad, where do you think I would choose?"

Rena told her confidently; "Abroad of course!"

The lady's soft spoken husband thought he would take a turn at the social experiment now; "If a person asks you Rena today if you'd rather be the person who you are today or a person less informed but more durable, who would you choose to be?"

Rena laughed thinking this was a joke; "I'd say I'd rather be well informed rather than more durable."

The couple looked at each other and smiled at each other endearingly, then May asked Rena gently; "So you would choose the easier path?"

"For sure!" Rena said confidently.

"It's funny that you are trying to help us when you have no idea that there is no easy path in life to be well informed. And it is only the durable who are well informed, because they are mindful enough to understand that they absolutely have no control over their own life."

Rena felt insulted, who were these people destitute yet confident enough to speak to her like that.

Rena was fuming when Kamal came back to his loft.

"What's wrong?" he asked her tenderly,

"I was lectured by this couple while I was interviewing them to be able to help them."

"They don't need your help." He told her casually, as he began undressing to take a shower,

"Clearly! They were laughing together more than any couple I've seen on a bench in Hyde Park on Valentine's day.

"I still don't get what is bothering you? That they are laughing together?"

"No… I don't know, when I signed my name at this NGO, I thought I'd be making a difference."

"What difference? And to whom?"

"Lebanese people's lives or at least ameliorate their lifestyle!"

Kamal got annoyed at this exclamation and asked her, "Do you think you are dealing with the combustible elements of a cheap novel?"

Rena looked up from the couch where she was hugging her legs for comfort. This was not the reaction she was expecting; she signed her name to have something to do and to impress him, knowing his nature of deep appreciation for altruistic activities.

"I thought you'd be at least impressed!" she told him earnestly.

"I'd be impressed if you do something for yourself and be genuinely empathetic about it, instead of portraying sympathy for all the wrong reasons."

"I do care!" she exclaimed.

"About what?" he asked her passionately.

She looked confused, it is true her ulterior motives were a little selfish, but it was shocking that to this particular man, nothing infiltrates his mind.

"Do you know the song Mack the Knife?" Kamal asked her after he came back from the shower with a towel wrapped around his waist.

"No!" she answered quietly, while completely infused by his physical form.

He took his phone turned on his bluetooth speakers and played the song by Frank Sinatra.

"Oh its Frank Sinatra." She said amusingly.

"Yes he sings it but it is not for him."

"Who is it by originally?"

"It's a song about Mackie Messer, from The Threepenny Opera, he was a charming and dangerous figure who was feared by many for his criminal activities. He is also portrayed as being charismatic and admired despite his criminal nature."

Rena felt there was going to be a belittling lecture after that explanation. After the song was done, and he was still standing on top of her, she asked him "So I am like Mack I'm guessing, if this is what you are trying to tell me. After all, in every song lyrics is hung a coward's heart. No?"

He burst out laughing; "Your world my darling is like cheap novels which usually include sex, racism, murder, perjury, inept cops, political blackmail, ass-kissing sympathizers, and hoity mother-in-laws. The world of Mack the knife is like the Lebanese mobs in our political scene, yet you just signed up for something that mimics the mob life in its criminal demeanors, only it is a lot more lighthearted and expresses its sympathetic and not empathetic mission in a tongue-in-cheek manner."

This was way too insulting for her, so she told him "I do not think I care enough to tolerate this sort of lecture from you anymore."

"Do you promise?" he answered her back, as he watched her gather her things to leave.

She ignored him and began gathering her things at a fast pace, she later began slowing down thinking this was perhaps just a witty, sensitive argument with every party placing their angle on the matter. But as she stayed on more than an hour after packing and realized he did not come out of his room and that he wasn't willing to take a chance on her. She closed the front door of the loft behind her tearfully.

Chapter 9: The Lebanese Mobs

There was never any doubt that Lebanon's political and economic systems were risky; as a semi-democratic, sectarian sharing system, with a laissez-faire economy that yielded little productivity, the pervasive issues of corruption and malevolent financial practices further heightened the precarious nature of the situation. It seemed inevitable that, given these circumstances, the bubble of stability would eventually burst, leaving the nation to clash with the consequences of its intricate and problematic systems.

On October 17, 2019, Lebanon awoke from its lethargy that had lasted centuries, the weather was warm and the soft breeze helped to sweep out the cabinet that was rotting of grandeur in less than two months of daily revolutions. Only then did the Lebanese dare to take to the streets without being attacked, as the dim street lights of Martyrs' square were perfect for the music and the dance parties that were taking place.

Yet, this festive atmosphere was abruptly interred in a pit of uncertainty following the resignation of the cabinet. A peculiar transformation gripped the streets, plunging them into an atmosphere reminiscent of a bygone era. Darkness, like an ancient force, crept through the alleys, replacing the once vibrant celebration with an eerie stillness. Human sounds were drowned out by the dissonant notes of tear gas canisters and the sharp cracks of rubber bullets.

As the days grew shorter, the revolution took on a harsher tone. Chaos festered among the free thinkers, and the guardians of order fled, leaving the sweeping darkness unchecked. The price of resistance grew steeper, lost eyes and maimed limbs became the standard, but the spirit endured, resilient in the face of mounting panic. Concrete barriers erected by the Grand Serail and the Lebanese Parliament blocked civilian access, and the once inviting streets of downtown Beirut now stood armored and impenetrable.

The anticipation lingered until January, a month that did not bring the renewal people were hoping for, but a new government cloaked in the shadows of the sweeping force that had engulfed the nation. The Grand Serail and Parliament, once symbols of governance, stood as silent witnesses to the transformation, as Lebanon entered a new chapter, shrouded in the echoes of its revolutionary tumult.

It was the dawn of the nightmare! A government that menaces with violence and death ruled as if they knew they were predestined to never die. At that time, glamorous downtown Beirut looked like a marketplace where a person had to make their way through orderlies unloading produce and gadgets, stepping over beggars with their famished children that were sleeping on sidewalks in a huddle, awaiting charity. Nobody on the street knew who was who anymore as the grand disorder came into full effect.

The Grand Serail on top of the hill overlooking the topaz sea was all safe and sound behind the fortress that was recently built and where all manners of laws and decrees were signed to decide the destiny of the nation.

While Covid-19 was spreading, a shadowy transformation occurred in the corridors of power. The once official rulers of the nation found themselves overshadowed by a new and unexpected force, the imposter government. As the virus tightened its grip on the world, this clandestine authority gradually emerged as an indispensable player in the theater of governance. In the initial months of the pandemic, the official rulers struggled to contain the revolution, but the imposter government, previously dismissed as a mere mimicry of authority, swiftly seized control.

The official imposters, once thought to be proxies for their legitimate counterparts, were now rendered obsolete. The true rulers of the nation, plagued by the unpredictable nature of the pandemic, found themselves relegated to mere spectators of their own destiny. The imposter government, however, adapted to the crisis of the pandemic with an unexpected efficacy that surprised even its staunchest critics.

During this period of uncertainty, the imposter government became the linchpin of stability, holding the reins of power with an iron grip. Fear permeated the air, not from the threat of the virus alone, but from the shadows cast by those who had assumed control. Original rulers in the meantime sought out loyalty from their communities by providing free PCR tests and Covid related medications.

In a world reshaped by the pandemic, the balance of influence had tilted, leaving both rulers and subjects uncertain about the true nature of their governance.

The first to suffer from all the radical negative forces that were taking place were the businesses that needed hard currency. They were pushed to revert to the black market because banks began lowering withdrawal limits and imposed arbitrary rules, like banning transactions on the US Dollar. That effected workers that had long lost the opportunity to extract dollars from ATMs and from using their accounts in any possible way. Petrol stations, pharmacies, supermarkets and hospitals, were the only functional businesses during lockdown and yet their quest to secure capital was unattainable. Despite the central bank's reassurance to guarantee dollars for firms that import fuel, medicine and wheat, the value of that reassurance was depreciating just as fast as the Lebanese pound. And so began the dawn of the shortages that led the Lebanese people to queue at gas stations, bakeries and pharmacies.

KAMAL'S DARK HAIR ACCENTUATED his naturally sanguine face, and the spring air was relieving his roughened skin from an unwarranted nightlife binge. There was still no way for him to shut down any screen that displayed news about his beloved country, even after three years of a lifestyle that seemed to lack any purpose. To him everything was acceptable except the August 4 explosion, it was impossible for him to understand why he was spared and his family wasn't despite being with them in the same house. The old Lebanese homes in his neighborhood with their sides shored up with baulks of timber, their windows patched with plastic bags and their roofs with cardboard, lay lifeless over the streets that only came alive after eight pm. It was a funny feeling for anyone that frequented the bars on the street, because they were less than a kilometer away from the explosion site, where fermented wheat dust swirled in the air over the heaps of rubble.

He did have one memory of his mother as she lay in the hospital bed with her limbs all smashed because a door fell on her, "It's ok, we will rebuild again." She told him softly. And that memory made him smile.

It had been a couple of days since he last saw Rena and he wasn't sure if he had lost the power of expressing himself eloquently that spurred her to leave, then again he had genuinely forgotten what he had told her because there had been a restless monologue running in his mind ever since he went to Laura's house and crashed her evening with Malek. He never felt he needed so much courage to do anything except around Laura. The magnitude of what he was planning on doing was starting to become clear to him.

He left his house abruptly and was almost going to slam into his next-door neighbor when he heard Malek call out for him from the other side of the road;

"Why are you in a hurry?" his friend ran up to him,

"I'm not, I was just thinking of something."

"What about?" Malek smiled at him widely.

Kamal suddenly forgot what it is that he had originally intended to do, even though for the last couple of days he had been making ready for this moment.

Malek stared at his friend who seemed to be occupied with his own thoughts, and so he asked loudly "Lunch?"

Kamal jumped a little as he snapped back to reality, "Umm sure"

They walked past a couple of old homes that resembled Kamal's house and went into a garden that had a couple of tables scattered around,

"Shall I call Haya and Laura to join us?" Malek asked.

"Umm sure" Kamal said as he scanned the menu on his phone,

In around half an hour the ladies had joined their favorite men.

"Where is Rena?" Haya asked enthusiastically,

"I don't know." Kamal answered honestly,

"What? You broke up already?" Haya asked, pretending to be concerned.

"Well that's a record!" Laura laughed at him, "I doubt I've ever seen you last with anyone for more than a week."

Kamal sat back on his chair as the group laughed at that comment, a sense of complete helplessness had descended upon him as he knew who he was completely enamored with and ventured to tell her the tale by the mute eloquence of his eyes.

Laura suddenly went quiet, as Malek joked "I think he's high today!" He put up his hand in front of Kamal's face and started moving it up and down then left and right.

"Share the goodies!" Haya exclaimed as she slapped his hand, which made Kamal snap back to reality again.

For the last three years, all Kamal could ever focus on was how to get rid of the Lebanese mobs that have been ruling the country for the last thirty years, lately it had been some days where he believed in the cause that was set out by the October 17, 2019 revolution, while other days not so much. There was no more evidence that there was a concrete solution or even a line of attack to accomplish that. But now today in this garden, what he was looking at was blushing, and that made him feel that not everything is guesswork in life.

"Details!" Haya exclaimed loudly which brought Kamal back to the present yet again,

A waitress with a bare midriff set their orders in front of them.

"You are welcome," she said to Malek icily before being thanked. Malek looked up at her amusingly, she was quite attractive.

"I love that about Beirut." Malek laughed heartily as he watched her take the order from a couple sitting in the back corner.

"What's that?" Kamal asked his friend,

"The way nobody bothers to hide their resentment anymore, everybody resents somebody else's; money, job, apartment, girlfriend, boyfriend, whatever, and they make no effort to hide it."

"I'm not sure that is a good thing." Laura said.

Kamal smiled at her widely,

"Why not?" Haya asked her,

"A little self-restraint never hurt anyone!" Laura continued.

Haya put down her fork and wiped her pouted mouth with a napkin, "So everything would be better if everyone pretends things are going great, things are right on track, acting peaceful and content while their country is up in flames?"

"Really? This is coming from you?" Laura asked her surprised,

"Seriously" Malek laughed agreeing with Laura and asked Haya, "since when do you believe in what you just blurted out?"

"The road to rage, people crack up when pretending so much!" Haya exclaimed.

"So, are you going to stop pretending?" Kamal asked her directly,

"I wasn't pretending!" Haya told the group.

Malek leaned towards her, resting his chin on the tips of his fingers, which were joined in a thoughtful, prayer like composition.

"Would you like to come over for coffee after we are done with lunch?" Kamal asked the group.

"Yes!" Laura answered quickly,

"Yeahhh! Its been a while." Malek said enthusiastically.

"Don't you live in like two rooms?" Haya asked,

"Yes, my refurbished loft!" Kamal answered.

"Where shall we fit?" Haya teased.

"Stop it Haya." Laura snapped, "It's not like you've never been there!"

"The only two rooms are modern, the rest I feel like I live in a jungle." Haya was trying to explain her useless point.

Kamal's family owned a charming courtyard house in the heart of Beirut, a dwelling with a rich history that spanned over a century. This ancestral haven held stories of generations past, echoing with the laughter of ancestors and the whispers of wars. A couple of years ago, Kamal made a bold decision to breathe new life into a specific part of the house known as the Liwan.

He converted it into an ultra-modern loft, fusing the timeless essence of the past with the sleek innovations of the present. As the renovations unfolded, the Liwan began to emerge as a captivating masterpiece, a testament to Kamal's commitment to preserving heritage while embracing the allure of contemporary design.

Word of the transformation spread like wildfire, and soon, women from the entire city found themselves drawn to the Liwan. The moment they stepped inside, their eyes widened in awe, and exclamations of amazement filled the air. The modern loft resembled a miniature castle, with a harmonious blend of classic and avant-garde aesthetics that captivated the hearts of those who beheld it. The crowning jewel of Kamal's project was the terrace, a carefully curated space that unfolded in front of the house; it was designed to be only open at its front side. This deliberate choice allowed the breathtaking views of Beirut to be savored in a way that felt both intimate and expansive.

"Can we look at the gallery?" Haya was setting conditions while smiling at him playfully,

"Umm sure." Malek laughed as he mimicked Kamal.

"Do you have hot water?" Haya was pretending to joke about it, but Kamal knew that she was genuinely asking, while the other two just shook their heads as they walked.

As the four friends ascended the stairs at the end of the barrel-shaped vaults on the ground level, a sense of anticipation hung in the air. Haya's hand reached out and firmly grasped Kamal's arm, her eyes gleaming with excitement.

"You know that the central hall in a Lebanese house is a national heritage because of its unique elements of connection to the natural environment," she explained, a hint of pride in her voice.

"Wow, are you an architect now?" Malek teased, smirking at Haya. He waited for Laura to pass him before closing the door behind them, sealing the group within the historical confines.

Haya, unfazed by Malek's comment, focused her attention on Kamal as they reached a colossal beige couch in the room. "If you fix the mandaloun, I will go out with you," she declared with a mischievous glint in her eyes.

Meanwhile, Laura found herself gazing down at the floor, her initial enthusiasm for this outing fading. "I need to go!" she finally said, breaking the moment and surprising the others. The abruptness of her announcement left an awkward silence lingering in the room.

"Why? We just got here!" Haya pulled Laura by the hand to sit next to her,

Kamal looked up from his bar that overlooked a beautiful neighborhood in the city, "Are you serious?"

Malek kissed Laura on the forehead knowing exactly why she wanted to leave.

"Yes I need to pay Malek back."

"What? No you don't, it's my pleasure." Malek was angry at her now, he wasn't expecting her to say that or use him as a scapegoat,

"ATMs are not working." Kamal told her authoritatively. "They haven't been working that well for three years now."

"The ones at hospitals are!" Laura answered him back confidently.

"So you'd go to a hospital to get money that is used for patients, to pay your friend that you see every day?" Haya was explaining the scenario to the group, and trying to understand her friend's sudden decision.

"Yes!" Laura was resolute about her decision.

"Ok I will come with you." Malek said,

"You don't have to..." Laura started

"Nonsense!" Malek cut her off, "People are getting mugged at hospitals."

"What?" she knew he was joking, but clearly he had an ulterior motive to leave too, so she accepted and squeezed his hand tightly, she couldn't help but laugh out loud at this impromptu gesture that made no sense at all.

Kamal put his hands in his pockets and he watched them leave as he took in a deep breath, he needed to forget whatever it was necessary to forget, but whenever Haya opened her mouth, he would draw back his thoughts to his memories again.

Chapter 10: The
Lebanese Demagogue

From the late 90s until perhaps 2015, the Lebanese would get into drunken fistfights after hearing certain patriotic songs in night clubs. Despite enduring a war, the Lebanese society never really grew out of this morbid atmosphere; in fact a show of brinkmanship was the spirit that occupied Lebanese outings, but that spirit was absent during the October 17, 2019 revolution. Most of the population that took to the streets got their degree among polite society, and by that, the Lebanese learned that their heroes during revolutions should be men of temperance and wisdom and equanimity, or better yet, women, that was why the Lebanese revolution was spearheaded by women, or in Arabic it was alleged as "Al Thawra Ounsa".

One Sunday morning, Kamal found himself caught off guard as Laura's unexpected visit took him back to a time when their shared experiences held a certain vibrancy. There was a time when, Kamal captivated by the spirit of the woman in Martyr Square, had discreetly captured moments of her determination with his camera. Yet, as the world began to brawl with the unfolding events of the pandemic, he felt the weight of the intrusiveness in those clandestine photographs. The revolution had given way to a world of illusions, leaving people feeling trapped.

On this particular Sunday, while he lay on his bed, contemplating the echoes of the past, the doorbell rang. To his surprise, it was Laura standing at the threshold, a true manifestation from the pages of his memories. As he opened the door, her presence filled the room with a mix of nostalgia and uncertainty.

"Kamal? Do you remember once we were at this dive bar having this blue Japanese beer, and you mentioned certain photographs?" she inquired, sinking into his dark, jaded armchair.

Kamal still trying to process the surreal nature of her appearance, responded slowly, "Yes."

"And do you remember when you said that you might write something about it?" Laura continued, her words cutting through the air with a sense of purpose.

He scratched his head, a subtle smile playing on his lips. "Yes," he admitted once again, the weight of those memories resurfacing.

"I'd like to do so!" she declared with clarity, a proposition that caught Kamal off guard.

Teasingly, he remarked, "I have enough pictures for you to write a novel." Not fully grasping the seriousness of her intent.

Laura responded cheerily, "Good! So will you give them to me?"

Kamal found himself caught in a dilemma as he sat across from Laura, contemplating whether or not to reveal the collection of pictures he had stashed away in some folder on his laptop sealed with a password. Most of them were of her, a secret archive that held a truth he was hesitant to unveil. The weight of his secret hung heavily in his mind, begging for resolution.

Perhaps today was the day he should finally lay bare the contents of that hidden folder.

She broke the silence by sharing her plans, excitement evident in her voice. "Malek is going to help me too," she said, "he is going to give me contact information for people to interview and basically whatever I need." Her eyes sparkled with enthusiasm, unaware of the internal struggle Kamal was dealing with.

Taken aback by her revelation, Kamal stood up abruptly and made his way to the bar. Trying to shift the focus, he softly asked, "Would you like something?"

She looked up at him and laughed, "It's 10:00 am!" Her incredulous response rang in his head as a reminder of the gravity of the situation.

Undeterred, she suggested, "You know what, we could all work together on it."

Kamal, however, remained resolute. "It's ok, I don't want to be a part of this project," he stated flatly, his decision final.

She playfully teased, "Mmm, what could I say to make you care about my project?" I mean, is there anything I can say even?" A charged feeling arose, thickening the atmosphere.

"I don't believe in the revolution anymore," Kamal confessed, his disillusionment echoing across the room.

She proposed a different, approach knowing all too well that he didn't mean what he just declared, "I have an idea, let's look at the pictures now. This is what I did last night, I looked through all of my photographs and this is what woke me up again." Laura was hoping this would be a turning point in their conversation.

"The Lebanese have zero solidarity, they do not care about what's happening to their own fellow Lebanese comrades, and when it comes down to it, you yourself don't even give a shit, because all you care about now is highlighting a story to make your life have purpose again!" He spoke earnestly as he gulped down a glass of neat vodka.

Laura was silent for a few moments, and then said slowly "You can't expect everyone to be as sincere as you are. I'm just trying to make a small difference. And in this day and age, what else can a Lebanese person talk about? I mean really?"

Kamal walked over to his library and brought out a small book, it was his own book of notes and scribbles, he sat next to her and she instantly took a whiff of his fresh scent.

"Here, look, in ancient Greece, Plato told the famous Allegory of the Cave, in which a group of people are chained inside a cave facing the wall and on the wall they see shadows, the prisoners mistake the illusions they see for reality. This is what happened to us, for thirty years our demagogue rulers had us chained while we lived a non-realistic life." He explained to her accurately.

She was looking at him as if for the first time now; his short-cropped, very dark hair receding at the temples, baring the smooth ivory skin. She then allowed her eyes to move to his wide, sharp shoulders, his long, fine limbs and then back up to his nicely shaped, rather small skull. Kamal usually smiled enchantingly but never to charm, and seemed to distrust smiling altogether ever since the explosion. Faint lines of permanent fret were set in his forehead.

She suddenly remembered a dinner party right after the explosion around three years ago, when she and he found themselves at opposite sides of the room, left out of the nearby conversations. He had circled the room and got close to her without her noticing, and then he began to talk to her as if he was a flirtatious stranger. She smiled as he was smiling in that moment but with diffidence, as was natural when talking to an ensnaring man, and so she took on the charade and played with him the entire evening, where they had exchanged charged looks and vapid speeches.

There was a mix of some mild formality in the way he was describing the text in his little brown leather notebook, but also an uncertainty in his voice, it was making her curious. She reminded herself that he is usually like that and that there is nothing to be noticed now that has not been seen before. So she moved away to the side of the couch for a little more perspective and it seemed he was making an offering of his time and his presence that had little to do with the book but, rather something to do with her. It was an offer made with a touch of frank humility that if she had decided to leave in that moment he would not have tried any further.

Her heart was beating fast, if only he wanted her as much as she wanted him in that moment, so she finally said "Are you and I trapped behind a curtain of illusions?" A hush in her voice, as if there and then and rather to her own surprise she had come on something in the world that was still to be absolutely honored.

"You are the only thing in my life that is not an illusion." He finally declared and leaned in and kissed her, not tearing himself away from her even for a moment.

Chapter 11 Lebanese Ancestry

When big events happen, it is always very important to distinguish between the morning after and the morning after the morning after. The meaningful consequences happen the morning after the morning after, when the full weight of the story asserts itself and the balance of power is becoming clearer.

Haya found out about Laura and Kamal a week later, while having coffee with Malek.

"Goodness! Does she honestly take me for a fool?" Haya asked furiously, "How did all this happen?"

Malek shrugged his shoulders; he wasn't sure about the specifics but he was happy for his two friends while having absolutely no regard for the details. Haya was angry because she felt deceived by her friends, and that was painful. A week later after the ultimate revelation, the pain went numb but she was still furious. She was feeling pure hatred for Laura, and realized that her friend perhaps has never trusted her and so the horrid realization of that was just cruel.

A month later, Malek, observing Haya's lingering anger, questioned her, "Why are you still so angry?"

"I want Laura to apologize to me," Haya responded.

"But why?" Malek inquired.

"Because it feels like she was planning this all along, and didn't even bother to mention it to me."

"Even if she was, which I highly doubt it, it's not like Kamal was married to your cousin."

"What a horrible creature!" Haya exclaimed, oblivious to Malek's attempt at reason.

"I'm sorry, but you're being completely unreasonable. And why aren't you this mad at Kamal?"

"Because Kamal was tricked by her!"

Malek couldn't help but laugh at his friend and pointed out jokingly, "You are crazy you know that?"

"I lost my job, and now this! I'm allowed to be crazy."

"We all lost our whole lives. Is that Laura's fault too?"

"I have to go!" she exclaimed, Malek nodded and tried to say something to ease that anger, but Haya desperately wanted to be alone. She could hear Malek calling after her but his sympathy for Laura only made things worse. Haya sped out of the coffee shop marching heavily on the broken familiar sidewalk that she would walk along with Laura back and forth during the revolution, they would share a bottle of water or a small snack before heading to Martyr Square, but now all of that was just a parade of ugliness.

How ridiculous it was to believe in anything. On multiple occasions they would be walking so fast towards the protestors that they would bump into new groups who knew someone they knew, like the sister of someone they knew, or the aunt, or the cousin, or the brother, at every street or corner across Beirut city. Something about these people would make the girls stop, it was their mood, a mood of numbness, sadness, hopelessly being let down by the entire universe, a mood a whole country shared with no exception.

It would be fair to say that every Lebanese has a complicated relationship with their country. The thing about living in Beirut especially is that there is nowhere to hide. Everybody knows everybody, and everybody knows everything about everybody, and sometimes all a Lebanese person wants is to be left alone. However, this moment is briefly sustained until they wake up the next day to check every story of everybody they know on social media.

There was this unspoken rule now, three years after the devastation, if something didn't happen to you personally; you've got business to actually complain about it, how else is the problem going to be amplified? There is a sort of layer of trauma in each and every Lebanese that old tensions still threaten to break through.

Haya now felt like the disgruntled audience who'd shown up late for the show and not the central problem that people should relentlessly amplify and that feeling prompted her to show up at Kamal's front door an hour later.

Laura opened the door and that ultimately made Haya fly off the roof. She waved Laura away with her hand;

"You did an amazing job!" Haya clapped at Laura, "You created the most honest, tender and true love story."

"I didn't plan this!" Laura's cheeks flushed with anger.

"Oh the warmth of admiration and subtle flirtation." Haya spat while shaking her head.

Laura had been in a panic about Haya's reaction because she indeed felt guilty about not telling her friend about it and that was why she had been avoiding her.

"Well, if you must know, I've liked him since October 17, 2019." Laura was finally admitting her true feelings.

"And why didn't you tell me?"

"I wasn't sure exactly about how I was feeling up until a couple of months ago and it's not like I didn't try to tell you."

Haya gasped for air, "Am I honestly this difficult to talk to?"

Laura pressed her lips and nodded.

"Thanks. Well. Malek mentioned something about how it was hardly your fault." Haya said haltingly.

"Besides, I never really talked about those things before." Laura explained.

"So am I just an acquaintance?" Haya asked her,

"No, you are worth much more than that to me." Laura was hoping that this would be seen as her last hope for validating their friendship.

Haya nodded and looked at the floor, "So we are friends?"

"Always!"

They hugged each other in the warmth of their shared affection and sank into the softness of Kamal's expansive couch.

"So where is Kamal?" Haya asked.

"He went to get his laptop fixed, we are working on a new project of narrating the last four years through the pictures that we took."

"Ohhh! Can I be a part of that?"

"Sure, after all you are a huge part of the story and can provide the most aesthetic background to the whole story."

"I know!" Haya said excitedly. "You know how many months it would cost to research all that, and I have the first draft of the events!"

"See! Not only can you write this, you can even produce the project." Laura told her frankly.

Haya began dialing her phone "I'm going to ask one of my previous colleagues, she is amazing ... hiii Karen, listen I have some terrific suggestions for your art project that you were telling me about the other day."

"Ah yes Karen!" Laura agreed weakly, suddenly remembering why she doesn't like to share things with Haya. Karen had a relentless penchant for seizing any chance to flaunt her shallow expertise and exploit resources for self-promotion, getting her on board would be like a perpetual shadow looming over collaborative efforts. Every nugget of information if shared with her would become fuel for her own agenda, leaving little room for integrity.

"I'm very excited about this, lets discuss it further with Kamal." Haya exclaimed.

"I agree. Would you like to stay for dinner?" Laura asked politely.

"Yes! I'm going to tell Malek to join as well!" Haya replied enthusiastically.

"I miss him, of course, tell him to come around 6 pm!"

"Its 5:30 now!"

"He lives right around the corner." Laura laughed.

"I'm sorry, I'm nervous, I feel like I'm at a business dinner." Haya admitted.

As the atmosphere gradually transitioned to one of ease and lightheartedness, Kamal entered the room, his expression was one of mild astonishment upon spotting Haya on his couch. Before he could articulate his surprise, Laura updated him on the latest developments regarding their project.

"Well, I was hoping to change into something comfy, surf the internet for something naughty, listen to music, have a glass of vodka while slobbing out and watching TV." Kamal joked.

"We can do this altogether with Malek," Haya told him flatly.

WHILE THEY WERE HAVING the "Midnight Chicken" at around 7 pm, Malek broke the silence; "Finally I'm eating this!"

"I know it's my new sacrosanct!" Kamal told him. "Better yet though is having it with a Flora Adora Hendricks." He pointed his knife at Laura and smiled.

"So how have you guys been spending your time?" Malek asked, knowing too well this was something Haya was dying to know.

"Early meals with no plans in sight!" Kamal answered him. "Other than to sit in a clean and quiet house, watch the light fade as we listen to the dishwasher sloshing while cuddling under a blanket."

Laura smiled at him lovingly.

"What is up with the penny-pinching?" Haya asked inquisitively.

"I already know her upbringing, current family situation, her intimate dynamics and her waistline!" Kamal winked at Haya.

"What about her workload?" Haya challenged him.

"Can we stop talking about me by saying "Her", and thanks to you Haya, you will make my workload much lighter." Laura accredited her new-found friend while being slightly annoyed with Kamal.

"Haya darling, I know you are more familiar with dinner and partying!" Malek teased her, "But wouldn't you agree that dinner and a movie and a bath or a book and sex, is way better?"

"No! You see six o'oclock is perfect for drinks because this is when the real gossip goes down, and you can drink them guiltlessly with better sleep." Haya said confidently.

"I promise you, there is something decadent about staying in with your lover!" Laura was trying to convince Haya.

Haya had completely forgotten how confused and heartsick she'd felt just a short while ago, she was feeling a little sorry for her friends' new accommodative lifestyle. Her shaking rage was completely worn down by disillusion. She had endured so much in the last three years that her life was impervious now to staying in and finding compromises to adjust to a sedentary lifestyle.

She was pretty much like the country itself; her inability to cope with life's heartbreaks amplified her weakness and completely relinquished any reserves of psychological resilience and steely mental health. She needed to be constantly on the move and always overly exposed to society.

"So Laura thinks that our strategy for this project is to gather all of our photographs together and encourage a narrative that is more inspired by the Thawra instead of a story about the Thawra." Kamal explained to Haya.

Haya laughed and asked, "Is this to assuage the failure of the revolution?"

"No, it's because we feel responsible for the narrative, and we do not want to misrepresent it, like how the media has done over the last three years!" Laura explained to her frankly.

"In other words, you also do not want to let down Kamal's super high expectations for everything." Haya answered her squarely.

Malek sensing a rising argument between Haya and Kamal subtly mentioned, "This is not a sweeping, romantic epic of four friends meeting during a revolution, it is not going to turn into a grand opera, it is only what I would hope it would turn out to be, a consumptive dirge."

Laura glared at Malek, "No, it's just a story, maybe even an academic one, where we make sure we do not abandon the essence of why we were all spending our days and nights on the streets."

"Exactly, we are not going to abandon the hope for a better country and a better lifestyle, and what better way to get to that than a repertoire of the events." Kamal smiled confidently.

Haya knew her friends weren't natural abandoners of things or people, and she had to guarantee her role in the project even if it doesn't come to light. She had to stay with the project in spite of her growing despair of what her lifestyle came to represent because of this revolution.

After the explosion, the four friends felt a thick guilt building daily, that they appeased by apologizing compulsively for everything. "I'm sorry I don't have milk." "I'm sorry we don't have electricity." "I'm sorry there is no hot water." "I'm sorry I don't have change." Were statements heard by every Lebanese, as if the explosion were their fault. Laura was still a little bit like this, but Haya a year later began to wonder if there was some sort of universal constant governing sympathetic traits. When she realized there was no accountability for anything, she decided to drop the sympathetic behavior altogether, as it was natural to become irritated by the endless delays in reforms and the unsuccessful protests.

"We should talk about compensation!" Haya looked at her friends seriously.

"We'll discuss that after the project is done, we have no money now!" Laura told her frankly.

"In that case I think I should live with you guys!" Haya told her friends in an even more serious tone. "I mean I'm going to have to go back and forth every day. That is costly for me and Kamal has a guest house."

Malek's jaw dropped and Kamal looked at her in silent bewilderment, while Laura shifted uneasily, her every movement betraying the turmoil within.

Chapter 12: Artificial Culture

In 2011, Lebanon underwent a profound transformation. What was considered a flawed democracy ultimately turned into an unprecedented ominous system. The devolution gave rise to a peculiar fusion, a supposedly free economy entangled with the shackles of tyranny. Unlike historical tyrants who demanded overt obedience through specific behaviors, Lebanon's tyranny took a subtler approach, insidiously infiltrating the foundations of the free market.

As the years passed, the grip of this unseen force tightened its hold on the nation's economic landscape. By 2021, the once vibrant core of human individuality faced obliteration. It wasn't merely about obedience anymore; the government, with a methodical touch, sculpted a society where the very contours of the self began to vanish. In this dystopian reality, individuals ceased to exist as distinct entities; instead they were molded into mere pawns within a larger, more worrying game.

The fabric of Lebanese society, once woven with the threads of autonomy and diversity, now bore the imprints of a pervasive authority that eroded the essence of what it means to be human. The silent transformation, culminating in 2023, marked the completion of a chilling metamorphosis, a society where the self was sacrificed at the altar of an insatiable and dehumanizing power.

In 2021, a subtle revolution brewed beneath the surface, one that is not marked by crowds gesturing in squares or overtly challenging the system, but by a distinct sartorial defiance. The Lebanese who felt like pawns on a chessboard were weary of a tyrannical power that seemed unyielding, found an unexpected battleground in their attire. Their clothing became a canvas for quiet resistance, a bold statement of both extravagance and subversion.

The embodiment of this silent protest materialized in a fusion of styles, sharp suits seamlessly paired with bobber boys' flight jackets and the unmistakable stomp of Doc Martens. It was a look that transcended fashion, becoming a symbol of street-real rebellion. More significantly, it was a visual declaration of freedom from clerical influence, and a nod to a desire for a world unshackled from oppressive norms.

In this new realm, a peculiar form of accelerationism took root. It was a philosophy that bound the people to the tyrants in an unconventional relationship, the belief that the only path to a better world was through a deliberate exacerbation of the current chaos. Revolting against the tyrants proved futile, and opposing them seemed equally hopeless. So the Lebanese embraced a paradoxical strategy: to improve their situation they have to keep up the habits that made things worse in the first place. It was widely understood, stretched and recycled that meaningful change required enduring hardship, significant pain and navigating through an extended period of suffering.

Uncertain of the duration of this turbulent journey toward a better world, the only certainty was that it was an arduous road ahead, and so the Lebanese plunged their efforts in relentless outings and lavish lifestyles that were financed by remittances and outlandish loans.

"Laura dear, you are so sweet, really, in ways you do not find in real women anymore!" Haya complimented Laura over breakfast one morning.

Laura smiled warmly at her, as she poured her friend more coffee.

"I'm sorry I act like such a corporate bitch sometimes but it's only because I would like to get things done in a sort of way!" Haya continued, Laura ignored her and went about to scribble in her notepad her duties for the day.

"We need to get out of here, Laura. I'm more relaxed elsewhere." Haya insisted on her friend.

"You can do whatever you want, nobody is tying you down to be staying with us 24/7." Laura remarked at her unequivocally.

"We had a verbal agreement, so I am not going to budge until this project is done." Haya reassured her friend.

"It is kind of almost done; I mean there is nothing really left to do but to basically bind it up into a sort of manuscript." Laura smiled at her tentatively, "We know the delays are not your fault."

Haya gazed intently at Laura, her eyes revealing a determination to extend her stay. "What about the new footage I am getting from Karen about the art galleries sprouting up?" Haya proposed, hoping to find a convincing reason for her continued presence.

Laura, however, seemed skeptical. "I don't know how this is related to the revolution!" she pondered aloud.

Haya rolled her eyes and unleashed her perspective, "Frankly, I've always found that art galleries become the retrograde cliché in both literature and life."

"You have a point!" Laura conceded.

"I've always had this faint suspicion that galleries promote average artists in a certain way the artists themselves think they are ascending to greatness." Haya continued, weaving her thoughts into a web of confusion for her listener.

Laura, visibly perplexed, struggled to grasp the essence of Haya's argument. Haya, well aware of her plan's effect, smiled slyly, knowing she had successfully diverted the conversation.

"We can even investigate the supernatural parts of the Thawra," Haya suggested, persisting with her diversionary tactics.

"You mean if there were any cults taking part?" Laura inquired, readying herself to leave the house.

"Sure!" Haya agreed, her mind already wandering to new strategies.

Laura, seemingly unswayed, confidently remarked, "I think the events of the last four years have been dreadful enough that neither art galleries nor cults are needed to amplify their effect on changing people's lives."

Defeated, Haya sank back into the plush beige couch, her shoulders slouched. Her plan had failed. However, as Laura reached for the front door, Haya seized one last opportunity.

"What about who manipulated the whole revolution?" She blurted out.

"What?" Laura turned back, surprised by the depth of her friend's question.

"You know, the people who prompted the revolution without being directly involved, you know the ones that cause the effected change with the least effort, without actively manipulating?" Haya's words resonated successfully as a calculated expression for her ulterior motives. Her question, though seemingly spontaneous was a reflection of not only her improvised rant but a reflection of every Lebanese's own contemplations and frustrations.

"I suppose this could be very interesting to add!" Laura agreed, intrigued by the new angle. "Placing the obstacles of why the revolution did not achieve its objectives."

"Exactly!" Haya nodded, a glimmer of hope returning as Laura left the door ajar for a renewed exploration of that shared curiosity.

Chapter 13: The Japanese Soldier

It is not healthy to be a slave to memory, ensnared between the irretrievable past and an impossible future. Haya found herself caught between the irretrievable past and an elusive future, fighting with the shackles of a single memory that bound her. The sad fate she could not escape was the loss of her object of affection, a heartache compounded by the belief that trickery had robbed her of her love. To Haya, Kamal's affection for Laura seemed misplaced, and she, as an outsider, was convinced she could discern what others could not.

Rather than succumb to the overwhelming tide of passion and despair, Haya made a conscious decision to divert her focus. The project became her lifeline, a refuge from the emotional tumult that threatened to consume her. While her coworkers shifted into the mindset of cool intelligence and self-preservation, Haya's commitment to the project went beyond professional duty. Her survival in Kamal's house became a personal endeavor, ever since the choice for survival became hers to make.

Much like the country she inhabited, she became a project unto herself, a testament to resilience and adaptation. As the world outside moved on with its cool detachment, Haya forged ahead, navigating the complexities of her own emotions and the labyrinth of her chosen venture.

For the past four years, Lebanon seemed to mirror the story of Hiroo Onoda, the country was entrenched in a stagnant position, trapped in a perpetual state of dissent and isolation. It was as if the nation had received secret orders to maintain this status quo, all while yearning for a savior from abroad to rescue it from its ongoing turmoil.

The Lebanese had successfully woven themselves so seamlessly into their surroundings that they became entangled, deluded, obsessed, and inexplicably tenacious. In this short period of time, the majority of Lebanese, whether residing in the country or scattered abroad resembled Haya, an embodiment of a population unabashedly resilient in the face of insurmountable cruelty. They doggedly pursued dreams that weren't even their own, only to find themselves ensnared in a living nightmare.

One undeniable truth lingered, a curse had befallen the entire nation. The circumstances of its inhabitants had become so shrouded in opacity that life itself seemed to lapse into absurdity. It was existence characterized by a purposeful purposelessness, a life where every action seemed wasted and devoid of meaning.

Living akin to a millenarian cult, the Lebanese held onto the anticipation of a salvation that had yet to materialize. In this peculiar state, they found themselves living in the future, where hopeful actions existed solely within the confines of their minds. The country's landscape became a stage for a collective exercise in waiting.

Kamal and Laura were waiting for Haya to leave the house and were starting to argue together about that topic more often than ever before. One day, while Laura was out fetching groceries, Haya had finished her bath and appeared before Kamal in a white satin robe that clung delicately to her silhouette.

"Thank you for the hot water!" she told Kamal, her eyes reflecting genuine gratitude.

"You're welcome." He didn't even bother to glance away from the television, his attention seemingly captivated by the screen.

"I feel so clean and fresh." Haya spoke softly, her steps light as she gracefully moved around the living room, the satin robe trailing behind her.

"Mmm," he mumbled absentmindedly, acknowledging her words without much enthusiasm.

"Do you want to go out? I'm meeting some very cool people at the Pool Bar," she suggested with a mischievous twinkle in her eyes. Thinking he is going to be impressed.

"How can you afford that place?" Kamal inquired, tearing his eyes away from the screen and looking at her squarely with absolutely no delight or respect.

"I told you I nag too much," she replied with a playful smile.

"Then remind me why are you still living here exactly?"

Haya dismissed his question with a flick of her hand, deciding to head to the guest house. A few moments later, she returned, her demeanor unapologetically bold, and she asked Kamal if he can fasten the buttons on the back of her dress. To her genuine astonishment, he tactfully refused, smoothly shifting his focus toward the bar. Haya persisted, attempting to draw Kamal into a more intimate encounter but again he skillfully deflected her advances, steering the conversation towards topics that were more kind-spirited and neutral. He kept maintaining a polite distance until Haya finally decided to leave.

"Phew," Kamal sighed with relief once she was gone, aware that if Laura had witnessed any of this, she would have been upset.

A couple of minutes later Laura came in through the front door with a bunch of bags, Kamal rushed to help her with them,

"I don't want Haya in this house anymore!" He finally told her as they put everything tidily in its place.

"Why? She has a lot of great ideas."

"She has no standards except for the ones that she creates."

"Perfect! In that sense she is more moral than you and I."

"Excuse me?" he asked annoyed,

Laura laughed and held his face sweetly, "She is consistently Haya, she is whatever serves Haya at any moment and that is very honest. She is always interested in what interests her."

"Mmm, you are right, that has a fundamental morality."

"Exactly!" she kissed him on the lips and hugged him tightly.

"I think we should get a puppy!" he whispered in her ear,

"You must be joking!" she pulled away from him, knowing that he is just being loving.

"Well eventually!"

"I'm going to hold you on to that." She hugged him tightly.

That evening, Kamal kept checking up on the guest house, in an irritable manner, and was getting annoyed with himself, he was feeling like a stern husband, when just a short time before, he had been the perfect suitor and figure of fun. Now there was a woman living very close to him and had knock-kneeded him turning him resolute and disapproving. Laura gave him a look that was in its way quite cold, yet deeply respectful and more intimate than any look that would pass between married people, or people who owed each other anything.

"We should be neither her executioners nor her victims." Laura told him softly as they snuggled under a blanket, "otherwise we will be overcome with madness." They both laughed and hugged each other tightly.

After all, it is madness to sacrifice human lives today in the pursuit of a utopian future.

Chapter 14: Napoleonic Code

Laura and Kamal went for a leisurely walk through the recently bustling city streets; the fading sun cast a warm glow over the urban landscape of Beirut, while the hum of the city's renewed heartbeat was filled with the distant chatter of people blended with the occasional honk of horns. They always made it a point to stroll along the cobblestone paths, with historic buildings towering above them on either side. Then they would go down the long wide stairs to where the restaurants and bars were aligned, because the scent of food drifted through the air, tempting them with a mix of savory and sweet aromas.

The striking couple's hands remained tightly entwined, their fingers interlocking as they absorbed the energy of the city around them. In a quaint neighborhood, they passed a charming café, with wrought iron tables spilling onto the sidewalk. The aroma of freshly brewed coffee and the gentle melodies of a live acoustic guitarist filled the air. Laura stole a glance at Kamal, sharing a silent understanding that this moment was a beautiful pause in their lifestyle that has been roiled with tremendous negativity.

As they turned a corner, a young couple emerged, the mother holding a giggling toddler in her arms, while the father skillfully maneuvered a stroller up the steps. The little boy spotted a flock of pigeons pecking at breadcrumbs on the sidewalk. His eyes widened with delight and his glee filled the air as he pointed at the birds. Laura and Kamal, caught up in the infectious joy of the moment, joined in the amusement. The couple knew in that moment that they had found solace in each other's company, their love echoing against the backdrop of their favorite city's multifaceted charm.

By the end of the month, Laura and Kamal had witnessed a profound transformation in their roommate that, initially, they had mistakenly believed would bring positive changes into their cultural project. However, as time passed, they found themselves growing increasingly frustrated with her. Their patience had worn thin, and they were officially fed up with her pretentious posturing, relentless self-promotion, the gradual erosion of social values, and the glaringly public nature of her promiscuous lifestyle, all of which disrupted the peace of their shared dwelling.

In a desperate attempt to reclaim a sense of normalcy and tranquility, Laura and Kamal decided to take matters into their own hands. Knowing that Malek had a unique living situation in a three-storey penthouse with a history involving pasties and g-strings, they approached him for assistance. They were really hoping Malek would be generous enough to consider taking Haya as a new roommate, given that his lifestyle might align more with hers.

In making this decision, Laura and Kamal hoped to not only alleviate their own frustrations but also find a more compatible living arrangement for Haya, where she could thrive in their project without encroaching on their sense of peace and social values.

KAMAL'S BROWS FURROWED in disappointment as he looked at his pal, "What do you mean no?" he asked hopelessly.

Malek shrugged nonchalantly, "You were crazy enough to take her in, in the first place, what does that have to do with me?"

"But she imposed herself, you were there! As if you wouldn't have done the same if it happened to you." Kamal pleaded.

"Thankfully it didn't!" Malek replied, genuine relief in his voice.

"Come on, you two get along so well," Kamal insisted.

"We all get along so well!" Malek retorted.

"You know what I mean!" Kamal slapped his friend on the back, a hopeful grin on his face, "Just for one week?"

Malek sighed, looking at Kamal with a mix of reluctance and affection, "Okay, only because I love you."

Kamal's eyes lit up with excitement as Malek reluctantly agreed to his proposal. The bustling sounds of the city surrounded them as they stood by the curb of their favorite snack shop.

WHEN THE COUPLE BROKE the news to Haya she wasn't sure how she would react since this was not going according to her plan, however, Malek's penthouse felt like an intelligent escape.

Here were the things that she liked about Malek; he was decisive, masculine, smart and well-educated, he had a sense of purpose, he owned suits and returned phone calls, he was more grown up than Kamal and Laura for sure. More importantly he had the maturity to recognize and address fun people, and this was preferable to the relative shallowness of a person who has never felt the weight of a real struggle. All the while he is protective of his friends. She wondered to herself briefly why she was never attracted to him? This was reassuring since she was going to become his roommate and that move felt almost magical in its timing.

Haya and Malek had something in common; sometimes Malek could be the teeniest bit pretentious. He made a big show of knowing how to select art work. He had a temper which was concerning for Haya and didn't suffer fools, not to mention that his sense of humor was a bit snide. However, after hanging out with Laura and Kamal for four years now, he ultimately softened his faults and became more soft spoken and kind.

When Haya moved in with Malek, she wondered why he was collecting classical furniture for his architecturally significant home. She immediately felt like she was the natural addition to his lot. Her presence in his life said what his taste in furniture and cars communicated: a refined understanding of what matters; clean lines and function.

As she explored the space, her fingers gracefully glided over the surface of his overpriced dinner table, appreciating the craftsmanship that went into its creation. With a touch of humor, she remarked, "Now that is craftsmanship!" expecting a shared moment of laughter.

Malek, though as a man, who took his furniture seriously, remained solemn. His commitment to the aesthetic of his home reflected a dedication that seemed unwavering.

Curious about the effort invested in maintaining such an exquisite space, Haya inquired, "How long did it take you to fix all that?"

"Still working on it!" he exclaimed, hinting at an ongoing commitment to perfection, even in the midst of the turmoil the country was enduring and the financial challenges that just kept escalating.

The explosion blew up his house and it has taken him four years to make it look habitable again, but even before that, despite the fact that he did not participate in the protests, he opened up his house for the people that sought shelter from the violence in the streets.

While the miasma of Covid-19 swirled around Beirut city, the confusion among healthcare workers and their tireless efforts to understand the virus were rewarded with a slow and painful toll on those who dared confront it. The pursuit of knowledge about this unforeseen virus became a perilous journey, fraught with unexpected twists. Every discovery seemed to reveal only fragments of the truth, leaving practitioners struggling with the harsh reality that what helped one patient might bring harm to another. The absence of reliable advice cast a shadow over their efforts, amplifying the challenges of an already overwhelming situation.

Amid the chaos, supplications for salvation echoed all around, but their apparent ineffectiveness left many struggling with a profound sense of despair. In the face of an elusive enemy, some sought solace in the embrace of faith, turning to religion as a source of strength and guidance. For others, the relentless onslaught of the pandemic fueled a darker path, pushing them towards antisocial behavior as a coping mechanism born from desperation.

The once hallowed rituals of funerals crumbled in the wake of the pandemic, replaced by a haunting silence that underscored the depths of the crisis. As the city streets grew quieter, the survivors found themselves increasingly isolated.

Malek knew that his purpose then was to alleviate as much as he can of the extra burden on sanitation and housing from nearby hospitals and hostels.

"I NEVER UNDERSTOOD how someone like you is friends with Laura and Kamal?" Haya finally blurted out what she has been hoarding for the last couple of years.

Malek raised his eyebrows at her question as he brought in a tub of popcorn for both of them to enjoy while watching a movie. He didn't answer her and started flicking his movie selection; he found the cartoon The Golden Touch and decided to play it for Haya.

"Oh cartoons, never took you for a little boy." She joked with him as she grabbed a handful of pop corn and made herself more comfortable.

"Very little!" he smiled at her.

"So I guess the point of the movie is that greed will destroy you and that the pursuit of wealth will cost you everything that is truly important." She looked at him and beamed. He smiled and put one leg above the other, as he decided to search around for some songs.

"That is rich coming from you Malek!" she said angrily, his quiet demeanor provoking her even more,

"I guess if you have the chance to be granted a wish by the Gods what would it be?" he asked her,

"Get my old life back, it was lovely!"

"Really, which parts exactly?"

"Glitzy evening parties, feather boas, fur stoles, custom jewelry, grand cars, living up to the moment." She extended up her hand while she recited, as if she were in a Shakespearean play.

"Ok I get the exaggeration!"

She laughed and threw a cushion at him, "I don't know, I guess just having a life you know."

"Well you know what they say, when you ask the Gods for a wish you should phrase it very very carefully otherwise you would have missed the point."

"If there is any lesson that we should take from stories about the Gods granting wishes, it's that the desire to get something without effort is the real problem, nobody can get out of doing hard work." Haya told Malek wisely.

"Great, so are you going to work for your goals?" he asked her feeling a little hopeful for her.

"No, I am going to hire a consultant." She smiled at him cheekily.

If Lebanon were to ask the Gods for a wish, in accordance with Malek's terms, it should perhaps be for a management consulting firm, after all if the country wants to get anything done it is looked upon by the international community as a willing executioner. Consultant firms however, will do the job for you, even if it's going to get their hands dirty, the escape from accountability is one of the most valuable services that a management consultancy can provide. After all the Lebanese government has certain goals but they do not want to be blamed for doing what is necessary to achieve those goals, and so by hiring consultants, the government can say that they were just following independent, expert advice.

Funnily enough this was Haya's strategy now; use Malek as the consultant to get to her goal of getting closer to Kamal. However there was something she was forgetting, nothing is for free, and consultancy services have very steep fees.

Chapter 15: Eastern Mondragon

After the pandemic, social justice became more of the mainstream mantra than capitalism; it became morally sinful for supercharged corporations to destroy the working class and the environment in their pursuit for shareholder value. Despite the formidable campaign waged by capitalism to dissuade even the consideration of alternative systems, it was increasingly becoming a challenging sell in both developed and underdeveloped communities alike. The winds of change were blowing, and a reevaluation of values was taking place on a global scale.

In Lebanon however, there was no one in favor for economic justice, not even the Lebanese themselves, on the contrary whenever the currency fluctuated aggressively on the black market, people were more likely to condemn the rebellions that ensued instead of stand in solidarity with each other and vote with their feet against this great injustice.

It was a bizarre thing, because the majority of the Lebanese people were reluctant to be in favor of improving other people's lives. What they were in favor of was accumulating their capital at the expense of the chaos and misery around them.

It wasn't a shock event, that four years down the line, the Lebanese populace found themselves dealing with a situation of pervasive injustice, whether it be economic disparities, political corruption, or social inequities. Their collective stance against this injustice had become intertwined with the fundamental concept of impeding progress on a national level.

The initial surge of hope and determination that characterized the revolution had gradually given way to a sobering reality, a reality marred by continued systemic failures and a lack of meaningful change. Despite the initial fervor and calls for reform, the entrenched powers and vested interests seemed resilient, perpetuating a status quo that served only a select few while leaving the majority marginalized and disillusioned.

The Lebanese did not understand that money being saved in their homes is not going to the greater efficiency of a society and that ultimately worsens everyone's life. Instead of criticizing the harmful treatment of banks with their shareholders and workers towards their customers and the Lebanese economy at large; rentals, college tuition and health care costs all rose faster than inflation. Despite the exorbitant expenses, the Lebanese remained oblivious to the interconnected web of consequences. The very essence of societal well-being was strained as economic pressures tightened their grip, leaving an indelible mark on the collective quality of life.

In 2020, Lebanon had the opportunity to create an eastern Mondragon. A federation of cooperatives based in different towns that would have unique organizational structures and democratic principles. The corporation would have been comprised of a network of worker-owned cooperatives operating in various sectors such as industry, finance, retail, and education.

Their business model would encompass; worker ownership, participatory management, solidarity which extends to supporting each other in times of need therefore fostering a sense of community, social responsibility that enables sustainable business practices and education that emphasizes the continuous learning and development of communities.

All the more reason to endorse such an initiative was the fact that the Lebanese people's money were stuck in banks, giving way to the adoption of a mutual aid strategy that would have benefited communities at large and built natural resiliency.

Instead a pretentious lifestyle was adopted.

Up until 2011, life in Lebanon was characterized by a reality many took for granted, like supporting a family on a single income was not only common but feasible. After the drastic shift that occurred after the October 17, 2019 revolution, this once normal lifestyle was transformed into a rarity and in 2020, the Lebanese people found themselves in a new era, where the conveniences of online shopping and home movies streaming pale in comparison to the fundamental desires for home ownership, affordable education for their children, and healthcare that doesn't lead to financial ruin.

The allure of a technological advanced and interconnected world has its perks, but the people of Lebanon in 2020 and 2021 yearned for a return to a simpler dream; the ability to build a stable and secure life. However, in March 2023, the cost of living surged to a point making it increasingly challenging for families to make ends meet. The cry for change echoed through the collective consciousness of the Lebanese people, but for some reason, just like how "a woman's charm is fifty percent illusion" the Lebanese continued their fibs of immaculate lifestyles.

The mystery lies in the fact that during 2019, the Lebanese understood that creating a better world demands hard work, a commitment to justice and a willingness to address the root causes of societal issues. Central to this transformation is the urgent need to tackle wealth inequality, ensuring that the fruits of progress are distributed more equitably. Moreover, standing up for the vulnerable and disadvantaged is crucial. Yet when the Lebanese currency dropped to an all time low, the call for a better world was somehow nonexistent and instead of building resiliency, the Lebanese people navigated the complexities of the crisis through a society that strives on the prosperity of the privileged that ought to be widely publicized but not to be shared with the less fortunate.

Naturally that led to the country and its citizens to accumulate papers from many firms and countries alike that demanded to have their loans be paid or reimbursed in one way or another.

HAYA WAS WORRIED ABOUT not being able to get to her nails appointment because of a protest happening on the street next to where Malek lives, and complained about that to him in a way that was so out of touch with reality, it made her look like a tourist.

"This is not the kind of thing people should say out loud." Malek told her attempting to nuance her standpoint. "We still live in troubling times, either the news is morbid or people have shit to deal with in their actual lives."

Haya didn't recognize people from outside of her social circle, "You used to be funnier." She told him flatly.

"I'm still joyful!" he reassured her.

"Yes, but you never joke anymore." She retorted.

"There is nothing funny! It's like we are officially being conducted for a study on hysteria."

"Oh no you didn't" Haya glared at him, "did you just mention the disease that is marked by diverse physical symptoms in the absence of a physiological cause, occurring primarily in women, to justify your point."

"Well yes, do you notice your reactions? How irritated you are? Instead of pretending that you have been on a round of lunches and cocktail parties at your own expense, why don't you just relax and stop nagging." He answered her back brazenly.

Immediately, Haya began to wonder if Malek had heard some unkind gossip about her. She began to explain that in the last few years with the hardships that endured; she was too soft and was not strong enough to be alone and handle everything alone, and desperately sought attention from people to alleviate this nuisance.

"Then let me introduce you to something that they call in medicine and you of all people should understand; called catharsis." He smiled at her, she laughed but was still agitated.

He handed her a whiskey to calm her nerves and when she spilled it on her white satin dress that she had recently borrowed from an expensive store, she screamed piercingly and in a manner that scared Malek half to death, leading him to wonder why she did that. So she explained to him that she was nervous that Laura and Kamal are coming later, and she wants to be all prim and proper.

"Great, then don't drink so much." He smiled at her reassuringly, somehow feeling sorry for her, yet still feeling uneasy about that weird reaction.

Malek was about to leave the house when Haya blurted out to him that she has no money anymore and that she just wants to rest.

Chapter 16: An Explosion

Where else, except in the interiors of stars, do cosmic forces frisk together? Lucky for us, seventy years ago an atomic bomb was tested and then later it was used to end World War II, the world experienced then the light of a nuclear explosion. (Pure sarcasm) An event that has left an ineradicable mark on human history and reshaped the political landscape by casting a long shadow over the collective consciousness of a world forever changed by the horrors of nuclear explosions.

In Lebanon we didn't have the privilege yet to experience an atomic bomb, but we did experience one of the biggest non-nuclear explosions in history along with the consequences of untold destruction; a massive chemical explosion that was caused by the detonation of approximately 2,750 tons of ammonium nitrate that had been improperly stored in a warehouse. The explosion looked like a giant mushroom, the stalk was the thousands of tons of ammonium, sand and wheat that were sucked up by the explosion, air expanded outward shedding its energy at the speed of sound sending a blast wave that destroyed houses, hospitals, schools and a third of Beirut city. A large pink and orange cloud covered the whole country, it lit up every peak and ridge with a beauty and clarity that cannot be described but must be seen to be imagined. A beauty that writers dream about writing about but may have difficulty in describing it adequately if they have never seen it before!

The debris cloud looked like a parachute that failed to cover people from ash, and convulsed constantly as it spread along the coastlines and hilltops. The detonation force had an estimated equivalent TNT yield of around 1.1 kilotons.

The non-nuclear explosion happened in the stillness of a summer afternoon in August; two ominous explosions completely shattered the tranquility, reverberating with a force that was felt as far as Cyprus. The resonance of a powerful roar warned the Lebanese in every corner of the country of impending doom. The shockwave even shattered windows in mountain villages that were not overlooking the explosion sight. Despite the ominous signs and imminent catastrophes, the government's official stance insisted that it was fireworks. Yet amidst the shattered glass and echoes of cries for help, the truth of exceptional negligence lingered in the air, as a stark reminder of a moment that would forever remain etched in the collective memory of a nation.

The city of Beirut sits athwart the Mediterranean; it is one of the oldest and greatest gateways between the earliest known cradles of civilizations and the sea. Trade was the gusto of this coastal land which ultimately led to turning the city into a checkpoint rather than a gateway, cradling wars that it had nothing to do with. With the financial collapse and Covid-19 lockdowns taking place throughout 2020, the Lebanese were like people trapped under the sea, with no air supply and no means of resuscitation. The only thing the Lebanese were able to do about their circumstances was talk about it, and with a grand supply of dialogues, the entrapment loses sight of a viable solution for a change in circumstance.

Just like Haya's veneer of social snobbery and sexual propriety, Beirut was a city that was once upon a time shining brightly, but the explosion exposed its insecure and dislocated individuals to the rest of the world. A fallen city whose family fortunes evaporated and has lost its trading partners that were essential because of suicidal economic decisions that were taken by the government in 2011. The city has a bad drinking problem; the only functioning businesses are bars inhabited by aging lulu belles who live in a state of perpetual panic.

After the explosion, the Lebanese were forced to display their dainty frail manners through NGO's to get people to send them money. They showcased a people that have never known indignity.

With Lebanese snobbery ever alive again, they mistakenly thought that buying time would hide the fact that they needed an immense fortune to stand back up on their two feet again. A vast majority of women depended on male sexual admiration for a sense of self-esteem, Haya was one of those women. There was always a calculated attempt to make herself attractive to new male suitors. However to remain attractive, not succumbing to passion is one of the main pillars for survival in this dystopia, and so a loveless marriage is the only solution to escape this impoverished situation that is tainted with a bad reputation.

In the aftermath of the devastating explosion that rocked Beirut, a different kind of explosion ensued this time, one fueled by the seething anger of the people. A tumultuous wave of discontent swept through the city as individuals from all walks of life united in their fury. The target of their collective rage was the Grand Serail, and it didn't take much time before the air was soon thick with projectiles and Molotov bombs.

The response from the authorities was swift and forceful. Tear gas canisters filled the air, creating a hazy battlefield where the clashes between the people and those meant to protect them escalated. Live ammunition joined the fray, transforming the streets around Martyrs' Square into a perilous zone. In the chaos, individuals who were supposed to safeguard downtown Beirut and its inhabitants, labeled as parliamentary guards, fired upon the crowd.

The consequences were calamitous, hundreds were injured, and the casualty count continued to rise. The violence spiraled out of control, prompting the Lebanese army to be summoned into downtown Beirut.

What began as a localized demonstration morphed into a larger, more ominous military operation, setting the stage for an extended period of civil unrest.

WITH KAMAL NOW COMPLETELY enamored with Laura and engaged in a healthy relationship, Malek was proving to be Haya's only chance for contentment, even though he was far from ideal. Four years after the explosion and after a complete economic collapse, Haya found herself at a crossroads with limited choices and dwindling options to escape the consequences of the decisions she had made.

The aftermath of the explosion and economic downturn had left her dealing with a reality that seemed increasingly unforgiving. Kamal's newfound happiness with Laura served as a constant reminder of the paths not taken, and Haya found solace in the companionship of Malek. She began to cling to a hope that Malek could offer a semblance of the happiness she craved because his presence was providing her with a sense of stability and support in a disorderly environment. Even though she was still struggling to acknowledge and understand that the current circumstances in the country had indeed limited her choices, leaving her with a complex web of emotions.

After all, the economic collapse had not only shattered the physical landscape but had also reshaped the dynamics of relationships and opportunities for generations to come.

In the wake of the initial explosion on August 4, 2020, the Lebanese government found itself struggling with a nation in agony. Despite the desire to impose martial law, a measure typically reserved for such crisis, and highly useful especially at the height of Covid-19, the government wasn't able to fulfill that obligation. The widespread devastation caused by the blast had resulted in significant loss of life, and the delicate balance between maintaining order and addressing the people's grievances was a daunting challenge for everyone.

The aftermath of the devastating explosion not only scarred the physical landscape of the city but also laid bare the systemic problems deeply rooted in the nation. Hope completely dwindled as citizens lost faith in the pursuit of justice let alone permanence. Faced with the bleak reality and yearning for peace, stability and a chance at a better life, over half a million young Lebanese professionals made the difficult decision to leave their country behind.

The more the remaining protestors attempted to bring those responsible to trial, the more the pursuit of truth faced significant challenges. Janet Malcolm's insight into the nature of trials, where the clash of competing narratives determines the victor, became painfully evident in Lebanon, and shortly afterwards, the Beirut explosion trial was abruptly truncated.

In spite of a series of murders and imprisonments in the months following the explosion, individuals who held crucial information about the catastrophic event were silenced. The struggle for truth became entangled in a web of obscured facts and suppressed voices.

An official order in 2023, shrouded in mystery and controversy, had led to the release of some of the people that knew about the events in 2020 and got locked up during the investigation procedure. Some of the detainees who were once condemned for their roles, now walked free. The absence of justice cast a dark shadow over the already deeply affected community. Questions loomed large, demanding answers that seemed elusive. How could those responsible for the ultimate disaster in the history of the country be set free? Why were the wheels of justice turning in reverse?

A haunting speculation lingered in the minds of many; the notion that even the most cunning criminals were not immune to critical errors. It was believed, at the crucial moment of their illicit actions, an unforeseen failure of both willpower and reason would usually take hold, replacing essential judgment with childlike thoughtlessness.

However, the perpetrators of the Beirut tragedy defied conventional wisdom.

Contrary to the anticipated lapse in judgment, it was not a deficiency of will and reason that haunted those responsible for the catastrophic event. Instead, a chilling excess of both will and reason seemed at play. While the Lebanese people's collective psyche was strained by the weight of the tragedy, the lack of justice in the years that followed did not absolve the guilty parties. Rather, it emphasized a disturbing excess of calculated intent and rationality that had fueled the tragedy.

The usual narrative of criminal missteps gave way to a disconcerting realization that in this instance, the criminals were not victims of impulsive folly but architects of a meticulously planned catastrophe. The resilience of the Lebanese people, tested by the absence of justice, only underscored the ominous presence of a deliberate, orchestrated malevolence that left scars on a nation that was already struggling to heal.

The collapsing silos served as a constant reminder of the consequences of inaction and the fragility of justice. As time passed, the quest for accountability remained unfulfilled, leaving a community suffering from both physical and psychological degeneration.

Chapter 17: The Webs of Deceit

In the enigmatic realm of Lebanon, there exists a perplexing façade that had always captured the attention of the international community. A realm where reality and illusion are intertwined! Haya emerges as a poignant emblem, embodying the complexity of longing and pretense that has long characterized Lebanese society. Like many in her country, Haya yearns fervently for love and companionship.

The explosion that devastated Beirut became the somber catalyst for change. As funds poured from sympathetic hearts across the globe, it presented the Lebanese people with a chance to rewrite their story, to extricate themselves from the clutches of a horrendous past and forge a path towards stability.

There is no judge but one's conscience, where the offender ends up alone and isolated, recounting the life and failures without any heavenly consequences. As sad as this may sound it is quite hilarious given that it is a widely known belief that is inscribed in every religious and philosophical book in the world, "Do not deceive"!

Amidst this influx of international goodwill, the Lebanese, ever the masters of illusion, embarked on a subtle orchestration of their image. NGO's, restaurants and art galleries became the benchmark upon which they painted an idealized version of their existence. It was a meticulous coup de theatre, strategically designed to conceal the darker contours of their past that is entangled in the tendrils of poverty and debt.

Behind the appearance of opulent soirees and cultural exhibitions, a silent struggle persisted, shrouded in the unspoken burdens of financial hardship. The Lebanese, in their pursuit of international affection, had fashioned a parallel reality, where the scars of economic adversity were deftly concealed.

After all, Lebanon was a land where the mere concept of a stable lifestyle was introduced briefly within a fragile window of thirty years. For the majority of the Lebanese, those years were a turbulent journey, marked by the relentless grip of random explosions, scandal and financial ruin. The youth of Lebanon bore the brunt of this turmoil with their formative years toiled amid the chaos of conflict. Yet as they navigated their present, a palpable fear lingered, a fear of exposing their vulnerability to the outside world. In an attempt to shield themselves from judgment and seek approval, they engaged in deception.

A ubiquitous tendency emerged, a tendency to weave illusions by constructing a more favorable version of the country at large. This was not an exercise of vanity; it was a coping mechanism, a survival strategy. In the face of the harsh realities that have defined the recent history of the country, the Lebanese resorted to the creation of a fantasy world, a temporary refuge from the pain and trauma that have shadowed their lives for the past four years.

This illusion comes at a cost. The fabricated stories born out of a collective yearning for normalcy, contribute to the perpetuation of the crisis gripping the nation. The illusion becomes a double-edged sword, providing momentary relief but also serving as a barrier to addressing the root causes of their challenges.

This penchant for pretense is also indicative of the fragile mental state of the Lebanese people. Their decent to lunacy is marked by an increasing inability to distinguish between reality and fantasy. The illusions they create are a manifestation of their deteriorating mental health. As a society that has lived in a once upon a time wealthy economy for a brief period of fifteen years, has ultimately fallen from grace.

After the war the Lebanese got accustomed to a certain social standing and now have difficulty accepting their current circumstances. Presenting themselves as refined and cultured, especially to the outside community, allows them to maintain a semblance of the social status they have lost.

In the end, this web of deceit that has been created by the Lebanese people and not by their officials has lead to the tragic viscous cycle of being trapped in a failed state. This pretense, while initially was serving as a means of survival and escape, is what is contributing to the downfall of a country, culminating in a poignant and tragic conclusion for the whole Lebanese society.

IT WAS A RELIEF THAT Haya had stopped blaming Laura for her misery, ultimately relieving the former of criminal motivations. Laura had taken the wise decision to stay away from her friend completely, because she knew and understood how much she was actually despised. Haya had become like a mad woman, at first it was subtle madness, but now she became an insane person with the deep power of deception which only insane people have.

It was by pure chance that the two women ran into each other at the grocery store one day.

"You know Laura, when I was studying to become a psychologist it was mostly to help other women, in the ways where life fails them, and I got so depressed for a while when I realized I couldn't help you." Haya immediately started talking, while Laura pretended to look for the things that she needed on the shelves carrying grains and cereals.

"Then I saw you at the revolution." Haya continued, "That first night, I thought to myself, that's it, I'm going to save this silent reserved girl. I'm going to save her from herself." She was speaking so fast and nodding proudly.

Laura was having difficulty breathing now.

"It took so little, really. Just the slightest push. And look at you now." Haya shook her head in admiration of Laura.

"You see, my argument was that if your intention was to promote good, the result would be good. I felt purity in my heart, and that purity translated to your present reality." Haya continued.

"How can you presume to know what's good for me let alone think I need saving?" Laura asked, Haya, her breaths getting shorter, shallower.

"What's so amazing is how easy it was. I did so little. And look how much happened. I even changed my own life. Of course I got worried when Malek got involved he has a tendency to screw things up, but look at us both now." Haya spoke reassuringly.

Laura's heart raced as she stood frozen in the aisle, Haya's words echoing in her mind like a chilling refrain. She had always sensed something off about her friend, but hearing Haya speak so casually about trying to manipulate her life sent shivers down her spine.

As Haya continued to ramble on erratically, Laura's mind raced with a flurry of emotions. Anger, betrayal, and fear mingled within her, creating a turbulent storm of thoughts. How can someone she once cared for harbor such sinister intentions? Struggling to maintain her composure, she clenched her fists, her nails digging into her palms. She couldn't bear to confront Haya, not here in the crowded grocery store where curious eyes might pry into their conversation. With a final glare of defiance, Laura decided to ignore Haya and turned on her heel and walked away, leaving Haya standing alone with her tragic performance amidst the rows of groceries.

Laura remembered going back home from the revolution one day, on the verge of tears, after being pushed and pulled and having onions held up to her eyes so she can relieve them from the tear gas effects. In fact there was a picture of her in the archive, one picture her head tilted down, then in another, up, as if she had actually absorbed a blow from the camera's flash. Her hair was looped up as loose hair fell casually over the creases of distress lining her face. The Lebanese women made the look of a revolutionist unbeatably attractive, and while Laura searched the photos she noticed something incredibly peculiar, what was missing in the day photos was Haya, she always appeared at around the time where everyone went for drinks during the revolution, wearing oxford cloth shirts with impeccable make-up.

From an aesthetic standpoint, Laura was grateful Haya's mental deterioration had appeared now while she was with Kamal, and not while she was alone, because she knew she would have been in serious danger.

Haya entered public consciousness around the same time as the development of the modern police force that was characterized by NGOs and private citizens. The lack of medicine available at pharmacies was threatening the wellbeing of a whole society, and industrialization was nowhere to be encountered. She was the proof that, indeed, the forces of madness could triumph over the forces of reason.

Laura was shattered by Haya's encounter, despite her mental resilience, she questioned everything. Even Kamal and the archive they had been working on along with the last minute arrangements that had happened, splitting the project between the three of them.

"Here's the thing you have to remember." Kamal told Laura that evening, "Some people are just tremendous shits. I know you would like to be soft about it and think that things can be put back together, but most of the times they can't. Look at Lebanon, it is the perfect example."

Laura soaked in the warm streak and coffee smells of the kitchen. She felt much better just by being close to Kamal. "So you think I should never even acknowledge Haya again, even out of politeness?" she asked him, more for her peace of mind than anything else.

"I think some people should be given a second chance and some other people should have the doors locked against them." Kamal told her jokingly, and kissed her tenderly as he wrapped her tightly in his arms.

Chapter 18: Human Satire

H.L. Mencken is an American journalist, satirist, and cultural critic, he once expressed the idea that the primary motive in politics is to create a sense of fear or alarm among the public. He literally means that by keeping the population in a state of apprehension or concern, political leaders can manipulate their emotions and make them more willing to follow or be led by those in power. The aim, according to Mencken, is to make the public clamor for safety and security, allowing political leaders to assert authority or implement policies in the name of protecting the people.

In essence, Mencken is highlighting a potential strategy used by politicians to maintain control or influence public opinion. By emphasizing threats or dangers, leaders can justify their actions, and in Lebanon for four years there was no willingness from politicians to implement reforms or a legitimate capital control law to protect civilians from this apprehension. It was a successful political tactic in the sense that politicians exploited the Lebanese people's fears to consolidate their power and advance their agendas.

As the clock struck 3:00 am on a chilly Monday in February 2023, Lebanon was plunged into a night of terror unlike any other. While most of the nation lay shrouded in the silence of slumber, the earth itself seemed to stir with ominous intent.

Suddenly, without warning, a colossal force surged through the region, emanating from the epicenter of a 7.8 magnitude earthquake that rocked Turkey and Syria. The tremors rippled across borders, tearing through Lebanon with relentless fury.

In the darkness, buildings swayed and groaned under the immense pressure, their foundations tested beyond limits. Sleepers were violently shaken from their dreams as the earth unleashed its wrath, jolting them awake to a nightmare unfolding in real-time.

As the mainshock subsided, the aftershocks began a relentless barrage of seismic activity that refused to grant even a moment's respite. With each successive tremor, fear mounted, gripping at the already weary hearts of the Lebanese. Time seemed to stretch into eternity as the ground continued to convulse, each passing second laden with the weight of an imminent catastrophe.

The initial earthquake lasted for ninety agonizing seconds, and when the tremors subsided, they left behind a nation scarred and shaken, both physically and emotionally.

Takbirs were heard from mosques because Lebanon was still reeling from a deadly blast in August 2020, the traumatizing fear that shook the Lebanese had a strong mental effect on their psyche.

In this indescribable moment of fear, Haya, who had been residing in Malek's apartment, found herself tussling with a blend of emotions ranging from anxiety to radical fear, to ultimate frustration. Her presence in Malek's space had evolved into a subtle pressure on him to take their relationship to the next level by proposing. However, amidst the fear, chaos and uncertainty gripping Lebanon, her focus shifted momentarily.

Haya reached out to Rena, who had returned to London after a brief stay in Lebanon. Their conversation unfolded over the phone, a lifeline connecting them across continents. With a tremor in her voice, Haya articulated the overwhelming sense of dread that had settled over her like a suffocating blanket. "It was as if I was experiencing my last moments." She confessed to Rena, her words laden with the weight of the event. "I feel like Lebanon had officially moved from being a techno-thriller to an apocalyptic fiction! Honestly I have no idea how the hell am I still alive!"

In those few sentences, Haya encapsulated the surreal reality they found themselves in. Lebanon, once vibrant and bustling, now felt like a setting ripped from the pages of a dystopian novel. The pervasive atmosphere of uncertainty and unrest had transformed the Lebanese people's lives into a chronicle, fraught with tension and misgivings.

Later that same day, the atmosphere was tinged with an unsettling nervousness, as if an invisible weight hung in the air. Malek's senses were heightened as he felt the aftershock tremors of the earthquake throughout the day, a brief interruption in an otherwise mundane day. Even with the tremors' unsettling effect, Malek had merely brushed off the earthquake the night before, retreating back into the comfort of slumber. However, beneath the facades of restfulness, guilt gnawed at him, once he realized the devastating consequences of the mainshock and its persistent grip that seemed to be refusing to relent. His mind churned with thoughts of responsibility and obligation, casting a shadow over his normally affable demeanor.

Meanwhile, as the evening approached, Haya felt ensnared by a sense of duty that weighed heavily upon her. In the midst of Malek's palpable gloom, she felt compelled to uphold the unspoken expectation that it was a woman's role to dispel such melancholy. Setting aside her own weariness and the weight of the day's events, she endeavored to entertain Malek, to offer a glimmer of warmth amidst the chill of his despondency. With a steadfast resolve, Haya stepped into the role, determined to bring solace to the troubled soul of her companion.

Malek appreciated her consoling gesture, finding relief in her comforting presence. With a sense of gratitude, he sought permission to express his affection through a kiss, she reassured him that such formalities were unnecessary. Instead, she gently cautioned him, urging him to consider the implications before crossing certain boundaries.

Despite her warning, there was an undeniable spark between them, evident in her subtle invitation.

Smiling at the unspoken invitation, Malek excused himself momentarily to fetch whisky from his bar. In a spontaneous act, he lit a couple of candles, casting a soft, intimate glow throughout the room. Sensing the allure of the dimly lit ambiance, he suggested they refrain from turning on any lights, appreciating the serene atmosphere it created.

She agreed and told him "Je me sens comme La Dame aux Camélias." He chuckled, acknowledging her reference.

"You know I do not speak French." He told her cheekily.

Her eyes widened, and she playfully continued their exchange in a mixture of languages, teasingly asking him if he would like to sleep with her, recognizing that the linguistic barrier might work to his advantage.

Amused by her wit and boldness, Malek met her gaze with a suggestive smile, acknowledging his understanding of her invitation beyond the confines of language.

In a rare moment of vulnerability, Haya bared her soul to Malek, unveiling the layers of her identity and the intricacies of her past that had shaped her into the person she was. As she spoke, Malek listened intently, his empathy bridging the gap between them as he recognized the echoes of loneliness in her words, resonating with his own unspoken yearning for companionship.

In this shared exchange of raw emotion, they found themselves enveloped in a profound sense of understanding and acceptance. For Haya, it was as if a discord of thoughts that had plagued her mind for years suddenly fell silent, replaced by a tranquil serenity she hadn't experienced in what felt like an eternity if ever at all. In Malek's arms, she discovered a refuge from the storm of her inner turmoil, their embrace becoming a sanctuary where vulnerabilities were cherished and fears were gently soothed.

A fragile yet potent connection began to take root between them, holding the promise of a beautiful journey yet to unfold.

Chapter 19: Dropping the Pose

A couple of buildings down the road, Kamal and Laura experienced the earthquake in its full extent and had ran out of the house and stood outside because they were afraid that the house might collapse. Parts of the house were dilapidated and it was just better to spend the night on the street. They weren't alone and actually sought and exchanged comfort with their neighbors, who ultimately dotted the winding streets in front of the grand Ottoman-era buildings.

Tucked behind iron gates covered with plants, the limestone mansion of Kamal's family, that dates back more than a century, was rarely exposed to the neighborhood, only after the 2020 explosion were people able to peek because a wall collapsed completely. The blast which left around 300,000 people homeless, left Kamal with only two parts of the house and he was utterly grateful for it, because the blast ripped through the entire neighborhood damaging every architectural gem in its way. It was the semi abolishment of the triple arcade windows and red roof tiles that Lebanese houses were famous for.

Kamal's lavish residence, with its division into two small lofts, belied the grandeur that still echoed through its halls, despite the ruin that had befallen certain parts long before the explosion. It was the meticulous efforts poured into the ornate doors, triple arches, marble staircase, and the resplendent gilded oval glass cupola crowning the stairwell that captured Haya's imagination. She found herself dreaming of reigning as the queen of this majestic castle, unable to resist the allure of its magic and illusion, even in the face of the generosity that Malek offered which encompassed a life based on light and truth.

The soaring ceilings and expansive windows flooded the grand main halls with light, lending them an ethereal quality despite their dire need for restoration. While the mansion's ceilings cried out for repair and its balconies and walls begged for reconstruction, its enduring grandeur and beauty, even in the aftermath of the earthquake, continued to captivate Haya's heart. Learning that the mansion had weathered the mainshock without losing its enchanting charm only reignited her obsession with the fairytale world it embodied.

For Haya, the allure of a realm where every room held symbols and scenes hinting at a higher existence, where entertainment spaces boasted gilded embellishments, was irresistible. She cared not for the historical tumult that had shaped Lebanon; from the collapse of the Ottoman Empire to its period under the French mandate to its subsequent independence and then to the contemporary nightmare the country was enduring. Nonetheless she couldn't ignore the parallels between the precautions taken by past governments to mitigate the effects of blockades and the challenges she faced in her own life because of contemporary blockades.

The decision to store grain and wheat within these grand mansions during World War 2 was born out of a collective effort to ensure sustainability and resilience against international blockades, this undertaking spoke volumes about the exceptional solidarity that was once part of the Lebanese people's innate culture. It was a gesture of unity and foresight, echoing through time to offer a hint of hope amid the trials of the present day.

Kamal's house was ineligible for aid following the Beirut Port explosion, unlike several other structures in Beirut that received assistance due to their public status. He embarked on the painstaking journey of repairing it gradually and discreetly, preferring solitude and privacy, to avoid individuals just like Haya. He was wary of those who might envision transforming the mansion into a commercial venture such as a boutique hotel, spa or event space, seeing such endeavors as a disservice to his home's rich history and personal significance.

In alignment with Kamal's sentiments, Laura concurred that preserving the house's dignity and integrity was paramount. They both believed that maintaining its essence honored the memories of those who had inhabited its halls. Rather than exposing its scars to the world, they found nobility in safeguarding its history, identity, and unique allure, recognizing that it's true worth transcended mere materialistic considerations.

Albert Camus, the renowned philosopher, expressed a profound insight into the existential questions that pervade human existence. He suggested that there is invariably a significant question to be confronted, presenting two contrasting perspectives: the pragmatic Anglo-American liberal query of "How can we make the world a little bit better tomorrow?" and the more existential French inquiry of "Why not kill yourself tonight?"

This dichotomy encapsulated every Lebanese human's life for the past four years, being stuck between optimism and despair, action and resignation. The Lebanese have a hopeful outlook, they seek incremental progress and improvement in their world, yet it is only in the field of materialistic virtues. They have absolutely no belief in the capacity for positive change that comes from collective responsibility to strive for a better future. They have died so many times that the future is uncongenial to them.

The depth of their existential despair confronts the stark reality of suffering, meaninglessness, and the ultimate futility of existence. They have found the answer to the question of purpose and value of continued existence in the face of inevitable suffering and morality, by persisting in any possible way and at any expense regardless the costs incurred.

The air was thick with anticipation as Haya's birthday unfolded in Malek's apartment. Kamal's arrival injected a burst of energy into the space, his jovial demeanor a stark contrast to Haya's growing sense of unease.

While Malek and Kamal were discussing Malek's latest additions to his art collection, Haya couldn't shake the feeling of being invisible, her presence fading into the background amidst their animated chatter. They asked her if she would like to join them for lunch but she excused herself to prepare for the evening.

When Malek returned back from lunch, he found Haya soaking in a bathtub, even though it was blistering hot outside.

"Rena is taking me out for dinner," Haya mentioned to him, forgetting that he already knows that her cousin went back to London.

Malek ignored her and slouched in his living room for an afternoon nap.

Haya was starting to realize that maybe he has forgotten all about her birthday after all and she began to worry about what might have happened with Kamal. When she emerged from the bathroom, she noticed that something has definitely changed and she became very frightened.

Love as a kind of fate, or curse, or judgement, and as a vector by which the universe distributes happiness and unhappiness usually leads to very unhappy endings for the people that do not appreciate its delicate nature. Even though Haya and Malek's relationship wasn't very romantic but there was growing interest from both sides as they spent more time together.

When fate, chance, powerlessness against circumstances and determination came into play, it was hardly a relationship anymore, but a trade transaction. Haya believed that love is an elemental force in human affairs, like genius or anger or strength or wealth. Sometimes it's good, but sometimes it's awful, cruel, even dangerous. To Malek, Haya was a tall, full-blown woman with a broad face and an easy going nature that only happens under somebody else's patronage. He understood that she needed him but she wasn't even offering sincerity in her demeanor let alone be affectionate at all, while blowing hot and cold with him, he had the feeling that he wasn't the only man in her life, and that would lead him one day to become crazed with grief, so he decided to look for a way to let her go in a soft and pleasant way.

He knew it was going to be very hard on her, but she was running against the mythology of love and that was very hard for him to accept. When he would look at his friends Kamal and Laura, he saw the romance in star-crossed lovers who are more in love than anyone can possibly imagine. He was hoping Haya would get the point to at least surrender to his love as a noble sacrifice and for a chance to see the relationship bloom. The only time she was seductive was after the earthquake and now a couple of months later, she was back to being crazed with survival plans. The fact of the matter is that nothing good would come from this unromantic prospect.

Chapter 20: The Power of Ignorance

Much of the evil in the world results from ignorance and not from malice. Haya does bad things, but often only because she underestimates just how bad the consequences of those things will be. She cannot help it, as a Lebanese she saw that in her country bad things go unnoticed and there is no accountability. So the population became like cougars on the prowl. This only leads to unhappiness because of the constant disappointing returns, and life hardly ever returns back to being good let alone move on naturally.

There is a mute and ironic reminder of how much some people's successes can depend on other people's disasters. That is why there ought to be a sense of respect for the complexity and power of circumstances. People's personalities are circumstances too, because there are limits to what people can do, and there are limits to what people can feel, endure, know, and imagine within themselves. The Lebanese have been hemmed in on all sides: driven in their soul to seek constant survival while living in a world that made acting on empathy unwise.

Haya just like most of the Lebanese, didn't know how she exactly got to that position in her life, she could not distinguish between what she was choosing to do and what she was driven to do. In Lebanon, the Lebanese relinquished their freedom too easily after the Beirut Port explosion, even though they struggled unwisely against their officials during the revolutions that sadly did not lead to any change. Giving in too easily made the Lebanese drift through life for four years now, because they suffered so much when they were struggling to change the laws that were governing them.

The stakes are higher for people like Haya, because she was not independent. She also did not submit to one of the predetermined possibilities this world offered her to be a completely conventional lady with limited scope. Her friends remade their lives along the "modern" lines politically and economically, because they could not force the people and institutions around them to change, so they attempted to store their struggles for change in an archive that will be a constant reminder for the next wave of change and how to build on it in a more productive manner.

"Would you ever like to have a family?" Malek asked her as they sat across from each other at dinner, to celebrate her birthday.

"What do you mean?" Get married?" she asked in a hopeful manner.

"Sure, marriage is a step to form a family, but would you be willing to put your life on hold, and have almost no improvement in your soul, with a lot of unhappy days, feeling mostly powerless, pointless and useless?" he asked her wisely.

"Happy marriages are the ones where two people are independent from one another but share each other's successes." She answered him, thinking she had dodged the materialistic perspective of the discussion cleverly.

Malek was so sad with what he heard. So he asked her: "What if there are no successes? Would you give up on the person?"

"Not like that!" she chewed a piece of meat quickly, "But I wouldn't sacrifice my time with someone that is not willing to be successful."

"Would you experiment with what will and will not work in life?" He asked her directly, having completely lost his appetite.

"Four years in Lebanon would make you not want to struggle, but they would make you want to seize the moment more often than not, and what better way to do so, than with extravagant outings and lavish weddings." She laughed, as she sipped a bit of red wine.

"Are you mocking me?" he asked her irritated.

"No I'm serious." She suddenly stopped laughing and was actually frightened again.

"So this is you reasoning of life?"

"Yes."

"How unfortunate! If you will only ever try to feel anything or take responsibility for something!" Malek spoke slowly and clearly.

"You think I have no feelings?" she asked him squarely, "and what happened the last four years is not my fault."

"I think you have feelings but not for me, and I am not looking to provide someone with security and extravagance if they cannot feel their own limits, let alone understand that responsibility is a never ending process."

"Did you try the squid?" She asked him while ignoring his rant,

"No, did you not notice I have no appetite?" he asked her genuinely concerned about her state of mind.

"I didn't notice!" she snapped at him.

She was so determined on making him her husband that there was nothing that was going to stand in her way now, not even Malek himself.

He regarded her with condescension, snidely wondering if she changed or that was who she really was all along.

"What is with the crone energy?" he asked her finally after gulping down his whiskey and lighting up a cigarette.

She wanted to tell him straight up that he is the unholy specimen she had decided will have to offer her the luxuries of travel to spectacular sights, as well as a complacent residence in the richest country in the world while other hardworking, noble, brave individuals went to bed hungry and stared at the same damned four walls all their lives. But she decided to keep these thoughts on mute and instead told him: "Can I have a cigarette?"

She observed how closely their movements matched and complemented each other, then remembered with envy the seemingly effortless simpatico of Laura and Kamal.

It has always been known that easy money corrupts, in Lebanon, the Lebanese had thirty years of easy money, all they had to do was put their money in the bank and earn a ridiculously high interest rate. Despite the warning of the Great Recession that nothing comes easy in life; the Lebanese relinquished thorough diligence, valuable standards and risk aversion, and instead abandoned financial prudence altogether and embraced aggressive spending. Especially after 2016, when the Central Bank engaged in questionable financial engineering procedures, the Lebanese were all too enamored with the super high interest rate on their deposits that they underrated risk, underestimated future financing costs and increased their use of leverage.

Naturally this is going to lead to financial failure, which leads to subsequent periods of stringency by everyone involved in the demise, like the government, the banks and the investors. In addition to all this failure, interest rates on deposits are completely abolished, which subsidize borrowers at the expense of savers and lenders. This exacerbates wealth inequality.

Lebanese young men had to learn quickly how to kowtow to bosses and how to manage women. Apart from the regular things they had to manage, like; how to be authoritative about mortgages, retain walls, mow lawn grass, open drains, understand politics, as well as search for jobs that will maintain their families for the next quarter of a century at least. Women had the sole responsibility to love their men properly.

Malek asked her as he prepared to hand her an envelope; "Tell me which can you live without, passion or food?" boldly staking his claim in a long conversation that seemed to be going nowhere.

Her natural state of ambivalence was all too consuming to realize that this was her make or break moment, so she answered him; "One thing that fairy tales teach us, of course, it that it is not wise to examine magical moments like passion too closely, better to accept reality as it is."

"Fine then, at the risk of ricocheting between layers of reality, because, without spiritual order or even pointed human purpose, life is just one damned thing after another, what is your purpose in life?"

"To live well!" she replied casually, "I am tired, I want to relax."

"Mmmm, in a world bleached dry of significance, the most immoral act might seem as meaningful as yours." He stated clearly.

He was truly sad and slowly handed her an envelope that was resting next to his arm.

"Is that my gift?" she asked excitedly.

"No, it is a ticket to go to a wellness center for a couple of weeks and there is also a bit of cash to get yourself moving once you move back into your own place." He explained to her quickly and sighed as he left her alone hurriedly before he could change his mind.

In that moment, it was as if she climbed from one life into another in an eerie second where she felt like a blank figure.

Chapter 21: Faded Gown

Malek's heart weighed heavy with the burden of the decision he had made. As he sat in the solitude of the empty room, the swirling emotions within him threatened to consume him entirely. The fragility of the situation gnawed at his soul, filling him with a sense of profound unease.

The nausea that gripped him was not solely physical; it was a manifestation of the turmoil raging within him, a testament to the anguish of letting go. He knew deep down that this was the only path forward, the only way to ensure a semblance of wholesomeness for both of them.

In the midst of his turmoil, Malek found solace in the belief that amidst the chaos of change, there still existed pockets of goodness, small beacons of hope to cling to. He held on to the belief that she would find solace and healing in the wellness center, that this would be a turning point on her journey toward recovery.

Amidst his resolve, memories surfaced; haunting reminders of the struggles she had endured. The image of her father, a humble bank cashier who had succumbed to illness due to lack of resources, loomed large in his mind. The thought of her mother, toiling as a nanny for a wealthy family, her knees worn from chasing toddlers across the floor despite her old age, pierced Malek's heart with a profound sense of sorrow.

Her parents had sacrificed so much, investing in her education with the hope of a better life. She had worked tirelessly to build a better future, to strengthen her character and nurture her spirit. Yet in the face of relentless adversity, her resilience faltered.

In the hushed confines of his sanctuary, he wrestled with his decision, acknowledging its gravity, but he also understood that she was not his eternal obligation. He wasn't destined to be her perpetual caregiver, just like how the international community couldn't be expected to continuously prop up Lebanon and be indefinitely responsible for its stability.

If only she had relinquished her pretentious and manipulative behavior, he would have loved her completely. She acted with a sense of entitlement, expecting to be taken care of and treated with a certain level of deference. They all saw through her façade but were willing to accept her nonetheless, however they became increasingly irritated with that behavior and resented what they perceived as her attempts to assert superiority over them.

To her, just like how most of the Lebanese now felt, life is absurd, because why bother? And who knows what is going to happen? However, what Haya couldn't bring herself to understand that not only is life absurd but meaning is fostered through connection and unselfishness.

Even with the horrors that plagued Lebanon, it remained a country imbued with significance. While perceptions of it may have been warped by internal strife and external interference, its essence persevered, refusing to succumb to the desolation that often accompanies conflict. Lebanon was not merely a barren expanse; it retained its vitality and purpose amidst the chaos and uncertainty. So it was imperative for the Lebanese people to fight in solidarity to encapsulate the genuine emotions that resonated within its borders, to capture the complexities of its reality and its eternal resilience.

Every living being on the planet is condemned to roll a boulder uphill and then watch it roll back down for eternity, but learning to roll the boulder while keeping a smile is the only way to act decently, while accepting that life will always be essentially illogical but never meaningless. (An analogy taken from The Myth of Sisyphus by Albert Camus)

Later that evening Malek emerged from the room, he thought he would find Haya gone, only to be surprised when he saw her dressed in an old, faded dress and had a rhinestone necklace on her head as a tiara. She had been drinking heavily and was talking to herself when he approached her.

"What are you wearing?" he asked softly so that he would not startle her, as fear crept up upon him.

"I just got off the phone with Rena, she just received an invitation to the South of France and she is taking me with her." She tells him the fabulous story excitedly. "It will be wonderful; I will have my privacy again and won't be ever again amongst swine. In fact Laura and Kamal called, asking for me back and imploring my forgiveness, but I told them deliberate cruelty is not forgivable and shut the phone in their face!"

Malek had no choice but to call the police, this was getting way out of hand very quickly. There was a hysterical vivacity possessing her that he did not know how to handle.

History raced ahead of the Lebanese people, cramming in a whirlwind of extreme events within a mere four years. But there was scant opportunity to fully digest these moments or engage in reasoned reflection. Regrettably, many failed to recognize their individual and collective responsibility towards their nation. There was a lack of concerted effort to carefully consider the words uttered and actions taken, with due regard to shaping the nation's ethos gradually.

It was and still is urgent not to lose sight of the crucial imperative of fostering restoration through mutual reliance and support.

Sadly, the contrarian thing happened, the countrymen where divided, with each bloc pledging loyalty to a certain international faction to survive. However that is not sustainable because no colonial power ever wants what is best for their overseas possessions. In fact, liberalism while depending on a foreign power is fatuous. And so for four years, the Lebanese have witnessed lying, humiliation, killing, deportations and mental torture, and in each instance it was impossible to persuade the people who were doing these things not to do them, because there was no way of persuading them, and so for the Lebanese it was a time of intermittent horrors and joy, that always left them with anxiety and irresponsibility regarding their own lives.

In Beirut city and especially in Martyr's square, one still feels that something is very wrong, there is a curious ruin amidst the lightly restored slums and shabby building facades with expensive stores, restaurants and art galleries. It is clear that there is still an unhealed wound.

Meanwhile, foreign dignitaries fly in and out of the country, collaborating with a parliament that seems to be always in stalemate, while the Lebanese are left in darkness, devoid of hope and robotically repeating to themselves; "we have always depended on the kindness of strangers."

The End

A TRIBUTE TO Vivien Leigh as Blanche Dubois for her exceptional performance in the movie A Streetcar Named Desire![1]

1. https://www.youtube.com/watch?v=dk0O0QgpmTw

About the Author

Sabine Saadeh is a financial professional, journalist and author of Trading Love by SJ Saadeh. Her work has been mentioned in multiple international publications, such as the Nikkei, Forbes, US News, Luxury Daily amongst others.

Read more at https://www.pinterest.com/sabinasaadeh/.